Withdrawn

KILLING BLOOD

KILLING BLOOD

ROBERT MCKEE

FIVE STAR
A part of Gale, Cengage Learning

GALE
CENGAGE Learning®

Farmington Hills, Mich • San Francisco • New York • Waterville, Maine
Meriden, Conn • Mason, Ohio • Chicago

GALE
CENGAGE Learning®

LIBRARY OF CONGRESS CATALOGING-IN-PUBLICATION DATA

Names: McKee, Robert, 1948– author.
Title: Killing blood / Robert McKee.
Description: First edition. | Waterville, Maine : Five Star, 2016.
Identifiers: LCCN 2016007148 (print) | LCCN 2016019326 (ebook) | ISBN 9781432832995 (hardcover) | ISBN 1432832999 (hardcover) | ISBN 9781432832940 (ebook) | ISBN 1432832948 (ebook) | ISBN 9781432836894 (ebook) | ISBN 1432836897 (ebook)
Subjects: LCSH: Train robberies—Fiction. | GSAFD: Western stories | Adventure fiction | Historical fiction
Classification: LCC PS3613.C55255 K35 2016 (print) | LCC PS3613.C55255 (ebook) | DDC 813/.6—dc23
LC record available at https://lccn.loc.gov/2016007148

First Edition. First Printing: October 2016
Find us on Facebook– https://www.facebook.com/FiveStarCengage
Visit our website– http://www.gale.cengage.com/fivestar/
Contact Five Star™ Publishing at FiveStar@cengage.com

Printed in the United States of America
1 2 3 4 5 6 7 20 19 18 17 16

For my dad. When he wasn't reading volumes
of the encyclopedia from cover to cover,
he was on the couch reading a western.

CHAPTER ONE

Nothing aggravated Billy Young so much as watching his brother, Frank, sleep, especially when Frank slept on a train. Rail travel bored Billy enough without that annoyance, and he pointed this out as his brother settled into the seat next to him and tipped his Stetson over his eyes.

"Hell, Billy," Frank offered from beneath his hat, "it ain't like I'm missing anything by taking a nap." He jerked a thumb toward the fly-spotted window. "There's nothing out there to look at but a bunch of sun-baked Wyoming prairie."

"There's always cribbage," Billy said, waggling a deck of dog-eared cards and rapping them against the small cribbage board he'd placed on the seat between them. Billy was the energetic one in the family. As far as he could remember, he'd never taken a nap in his life, and he was quick to admit that he resented anyone who did. "Who knows," Billy added, "maybe your bad luck has changed, and this'll give you a chance to get even."

Four days earlier the boys had left their ranch at the foot of Casper Mountain to travel down to the capital to see the sights. In that four days Frank had lost twelve dollars and fifty-two cents playing cribbage.

"We'll be back home in an hour or less, so you don't have much time to recoup your extensive losses." Billy had always enjoyed teasing Frank—at least he had since that growth spurt back when he was seventeen. Once Billy hit six-foot-two and a

7

couple of hundred pounds, his older brother had stopped beating the hell out of him and had taken to ignoring all of Billy's gibes.

That was what Frank did now. He answered Billy's challenge for a game of cards by sliding down farther into his seat and folding his arms across his chest.

Billy muttered a curse. It was frustrating to sit. He needed something to do, and a hand of cards was just the thing. He had loved the game of cribbage ever since he'd gotten his first board as a Christmas present back when he was a kid.

He turned to three men sitting across the aisle. They were a surly-looking bunch. Although they all three sat in the same group of seats, they seemed to be as apart from one another as they were from the rest of the passengers.

The smallest of these three sat next to the window fiddling with the frayed threads on the cuff of his shirt. Sitting next to him was the leader of the group. This man held a long-bladed jack knife and was shaving slivers of black dirt from beneath his fingernails. The third man sat by himself across from these two. He had his feet propped on the seat next to him and was eating a large white onion—crunching into the thing like it was an apple. The smell was pungent even where Billy sat.

"How 'bout you gents?" Billy asked. "Anybody feel up to a game?" The onion-eater ignored him. The small man with the frayed cuffs turned in Billy's direction but didn't respond. The one with the knife lifted his eyes and took Billy in. He was a large man. Even with them both sitting, Billy could tell the man was bigger than he was. He wore a white shirt and a handsome black leather vest. After a bit he smiled, showing a set of square teeth as white as his shirt. "Is that a pinochle deck?" he asked.

"Nah," Billy said, "just a regular one."

The man scratched the back of his hand with the knife blade, leaving tiny white scuff marks. "I like pinochle decks," the man said. "I played poker once with a pinochle deck. Had me some damned fine hands."

The man's smile was gone, but Billy guessed he was making a joke—or trying to, anyway, so he laughed. "Yep, I bet you did. Care to use this regular deck here to play some penny-a-point cribbage?"

The man shook his head and went back to his nails. "Not interested," he said.

Billy could tell by the tone that there was no need to push it. He shrugged and glanced around.

Toward the rear of the car sat a couple of newlyweds. They cooed at each other like love birds and looked to have interests that did not include cribbage.

An older man wearing a broad hat sat two rows in front of the newlyweds. He might have been a likely prospect except for the half-empty pint of whiskey in his hand and the glassy look in his eyes.

The only other person on board was a middle-aged man in a business suit who sat at the front of the car. Billy pushed himself up from the seat and started down the narrow aisle toward the fancy-dresser in front, but before he'd taken a step, the man who had played poker with a pinochle deck said, "All right, boys, I figure now's as good a time as any," and with that, the onion-eater rose from his seat and blocked Billy's path.

"Hold it," he said in a lazy drawl that sounded as though it came straight from Arkansas. Billy slowed but didn't stop until the man pulled a hammerless Iver Johnson and shoved the talking end into Billy's face.

For one of the few times in his life, Billy Young could come up with nothing to say. All he could do was stare into the dark maw of that pistol.

"How old are you, boy?" asked the leader. As he came up from his seat, he folded his knife and dropped it into his pocket.

The man who held the gun gave Billy a yellow-toothed grin. His breath reeked of onion, but Billy's spinning brain only half logged that fact. "What?" Billy asked.

"I said, how old are you?"

The man with the gun touched the muzzle to a spot between Billy's eyebrows. The rest of the passengers sat silent and watched. At least they all watched except for Frank. Frank was a man who was quick to sleep, and he had already nodded off.

Billy swallowed hard and said, "Nineteen, sir." He called the man "sir" because he figured being polite in this situation couldn't hurt. "I was born in seventy-two, and yesterday was my birthday. My brother and I took this train ride down to Cheyenne to celebrate."

The leader of the group lifted the Colt from the holster on Billy's hip. "Well, happy birthday, kid. If you want to live to see another one," he said, tucking Billy's gun into his belt, "you best do as you're told."

"Yes, sir," Billy said. "I will never give you a problem. Wouldn't think of it."

The small man who had been sitting by the window stood, pulled his own gun, and headed for the rear of the car. On his way by, he grabbed the older man by the vest and lifted him out of his chair. "Get outta there," he said, and gave him a shove.

"Hey," said the man as he bounced off a seat and landed on the floor, his bottle spinning out of his hand. He tried to get up but didn't look to be too steady on his feet even before the shove. "What's this all about, anyhow?"

The small man answered with the sole of his boot, kicking the man between the legs and knocking him back to the floor. The man gasped and rolled onto his side. With that, the small man grabbed a handful of the long, white hair that flowed from beneath the man's hat and dragged him to the rear of the car. He then came back to the newlyweds, took the young woman's arm, and jerked her from the seat.

She cried out and took a swing at the little man. The man ducked and gave her a push. When he did, the young woman's husband came over the seat at the man and between clenched teeth, the newlywed growled, "You son of a bitch." Before he could get out the last of his curse, the small man swung his pistol, bringing the barrel hard across the young man's jaw. With wide eyes, the man was knocked back, blood washing down his neck and over his shirt collar.

"Jimmy," the woman screamed. She tried to go to him, but the small man stopped her.

The noise finally woke Frank, and he sat, pushing his hat up a notch on his forehead. Before his eyes could focus, the onion-eater stuck the hammerless in his face and demanded in a hard voice, "Hand me your shooter, mister, or die."

Frank cut his eyes to his brother and glanced down at Billy's empty holster. With a confused look, he pulled his gun and handed it over.

"That's fine," the man said with a smile. "That's fine. Now you two get on back there with the rest."

Frank led the way down the aisle. When they came to the injured newlywed, he helped him out of his seat. "Come on," Frank said. "Let's get back here, and I'll take a look at that cut."

The small man jeered. "By God, would ya look at that? We got us a good S'maryton here." He was having himself a hearty laugh, but when Frank's gaze met the man's dull gray eyes, the man moved back a step to let them pass.

At the front of the car, the one Billy figured for the leader moved toward the man in the business suit. "You," he said, jabbing his thumb over his shoulder, "get back there." Without a word, the man scampered to the rear of the car.

The leader snapped his fingers and pointed to the onion

11

man. "Take care of the engineer and the fireman." He turned to the smaller man. "You, get the conductor and brakeman." He lifted his own piece from a holster he wore low on his right hip. It was tied to his thigh with a leather thong. "I'll keep an eye on these good folks. Now get going." The two men left the car.

Frank pulled his bandana from around his neck and held it to the young man's face. A flap of skin hung from the newly-wed's jaw, and Billy could see white bone peek through the red flesh.

"Your friend's pretty quick to swing his pistol on an unarmed man, ain't he?" Frank asked.

"He's quick to pull the trigger, too," the man advised. "You'd do well to keep that in mind."

In less than five minutes, the train slowed and lurched to a stop. The man with the gun said, "File out, now, folks, all of you."

The passengers did as they were told.

Once they were outside, the onion-eater and the small man, both with their guns drawn, approached from opposite directions. The small man was herding two men along. The onion-eater had rounded up only one.

"I got my two," shouted the small man. "It was easy as pie." With his open hand, he gave the man wearing a conductor's uniform a smack on the back of his head, knocking the man's cap into the dirt.

"I had to kill the fireman," the onion-eater explained. "He went for a shotgun he had propped up against the wall of the locomotive. I got the engineer, though," he said with some pride.

"You three," said the leader to the trainmen, "get over with the others." To his men he said, "Watch them while I get the strong box."

"Why, sure," said the onion-eater with a smile. He pulled a plug of tobacco out of his shirt pocket and bit off a chew. Billy hoped the tobacco could temper the man's rancid breath.

"We'd be glad to watch 'em," said the small man. " 'Specially this un." He reached over and twirled a strand of the young woman's blond hair around his index finger. She offered him a hard look and slapped his hand away. When she did, the small man giggled. "I think I'll get me some of this before we're done," he said, and made kissing sounds.

The young woman sent the little man an icy look. The onion man thought that was funny. "Look at that," he said. "Why, I believe she's about to gag. Could it be she don't find you appealing?"

"She will," said the small man. "She'll be a-beggin' me to love 'er." He bent close to her ear and whispered. The woman's eyes widened and the little man laughed. He didn't wear a hat, and shocks of greasy hair stuck out from the sides of his head. He reached up and tucked them behind his ears in an odd primping gesture.

"You pig," said the woman's husband. He held Frank's now soggy bandana to the side of his face. "You touch her and I'll kill you."

"Hoo-wee," shouted the onion man. "You best be careful. I don't think her husband there's gonna wanna share."

The little man looked up into the newlywed's face. "Is that right? Are you one of them selfish sorts a-fellas that likes to keep the best cuts fer yersef?"

It was clear the young husband was in pain, but he raised himself to his full height, which brought him a good eight inches above the small man. His eyes were slits, and he said through lips so thin they seemed to have disappeared, "I promise, you son of a bitch, if you so much as speak to my wife again, I'll kill you, and you're gonna die a hard death."

"I don't think so, mister," the little man said, and he lifted his pistol and blew off the top of the young man's head.

The woman screamed and dropped to where her husband had fallen. At first she screamed his name over and over, but that soon changed into nothing more than guttural wails, sounds that were impossible to understand.

Frank started for the small man, but the man turned the gun on him and Frank pulled up short.

"You gonna hop, rabbit?" the little man asked. When Frank didn't respond, he said, "I didn't think so. Now get your ass back there with the others." To the woman who was cradling her dead husband, he said, "You be careful, now. Don't you be gettin' all bloody, ya hear? If there's anythin' I hate, it's a bloody woman."

Onion man laughed at that one and slapped his knee. "I swear to God, you do beat all. You really do."

"What's going on out there?" the leader called from the doorway of the next car down the line.

"I had to kill me one of 'em, boss. That's all," the small man called back. "The fella was makin' threats against my very life."

"Get over here, both of you, and help me with this strong box."

The small man shoved his pistol back into his holster and strutted over to where the man he called boss was trying to heft a steel box through the door. Keeping his eyes on the passengers, the onion-eater backed over to the car.

"Here, give me a hand," said the leader. He and the small man lifted the box down.

"Golly," the small man said with a grunt. "She's a heavy one, ain't she? I bet it's full-a twenty-dollar gold pieces. Double Eagles. Don't you bet it is, huh?"

"Shut up and get that box open. You," he said to the onion man. "Get back in that car and bring out the mail bag. We'll take it, too. Once that's done, get down to the stock car and fetch our horses."

The boss kept an eye on the passengers as the small man went about banging a rock against the padlock. As the two men busied themselves, Frank and Billy tried to comfort the young woman. Her screams had stopped, but she still sat in the dirt holding her husband's lifeless body. She stared at something far enough away; Billy knew only she could see it.

"These fellas are bad," Frank whispered to the others. "They ain't just your usual train robbers. Has anyone ever seen these men before?"

They hadn't.

The man in the business suit, who had boarded the train at its last stop in Probity, licked his lips and asked, "Wh-what're we going to do?"

"I'll tell ya what I'm gonna do," said the conductor. "I'm getting the hell out of here. That's what."

"Me too," agreed the brakeman. He had a long handlebar mustache he seemed to have trouble keeping his hands off of. "You saw how he shot that boy down. He just shot him *down.*"

"If you fellas are planning on making a run for it," Billy said, "you don't stand a chance." He looked out at the terrain. They were on a rise that eventually led down to the river and a line of cottonwood trees, but that was more than six hundred yards away. Between the train and the river there was nothing but dry prairie grass and sage brush, none of it any taller than a jack rabbit. "You got no cover," Billy added. "You boys'd be shot before you made it twenty feet."

"All they got is pistols," said the conductor. He tapped the side of his nose and motioned with his eyes toward the two men working on the strong box. "The big one givin' all the orders is the only one that ever bothers to look this way, and he ain't even holding his gun. It's stuck down in his holster. If we make a run for it, we'll be moving targets, and if we can get a big enough jump on 'em, hell, we could be out of range before they got off a decent shot."

"I think he's right," agreed the brakeman. He gave the tip of his mustache a twist. "I really do." His eyes had a solid set to them, but there was a quiver low in his voice.

Billy shook his head and repeated, "You don't stand a chance."

"I'm gonna give 'er a try," said the conductor, and with a little smile, he added, "When I was a boy, I could run like the wind."

The brakeman didn't share his smile but said in a voice that was stone-serious, "I guess I weren't never much of a runner, but I figure if there's a couple a fellas shootin' at me, I could move as fast as the next man."

"Anybody else?" whispered the conductor. No one answered. He looked over at the engineer. "Felix, how 'bout you?"

The engineer gave his head a quick shake. "I fear these men're going to kill us before they're through," he said, "but I reckon I'm not going to guarantee it by running like that." He nodded toward Billy. "I figure this young fella has it right." He cleared his throat and looked down at his heavy, greasy shoes. "Besides," he added, "I got me a little boy back home." At first that comment about his boy didn't seem to make any sense to Billy, but on a second thought he guessed it did.

The conductor let out a breath. It was clear he had hoped his friend would come along.

"If your minds are set on doing this," Frank said, "I think you ought to wait until he's not looking and try to sneak out as far as you can before you make a break for it. When you start to run, run as far apart as you can and try to stay low."

The conductor nodded. "Makes sense, friend." He looked at the brakeman. "You ready to do it?" he asked.

The man's Adam's apple bobbed. "I reckon I am."

The two men waited until the big man turned his attention

to the little one trying to open the box, and as quietly as they could, they crouched and scuttled away from the others. As they left, the brakeman took a quick glance back toward the outlaws working on the strong box, but the conductor kept his head aimed right at the river and the cover of the trees.

"Damn, boss, there ain't much to this mail bag," said the onion-eater as he came to the open doorway of the boxcar. "You think it's even worth the trouble?" As he said it, he looked up and saw the conductor and the brakeman. "Goddamn it," he shouted. "Two of 'em's gettin' away." He dropped the mailbag, pulled the hammerless, and fired off a shot.

The two men were running now with everything they had, and the onion-eater's shot went wide.

The leader, who had been leaned over watching the small man work, came up straight, and as he rose, he said with a smile, "Nah, they ain't."

Before Billy could blink, the man's six-gun was in his fist, and it barked off a shot that dropped the brakeman in full stride. The outlaw leader raised his gun a little higher and squeezed off a shot that flattened the conductor.

"Hot damn," shouted the small man jumping to his feet. "Nice shootin', boss." He ran to the two men. Pointing at the conductor, he called back, "That un yonder's deader'n hell. Clean shot to the back of the head." He walked over to the brakeman. "This un here's still wigglin' some." He pulled his gun and fired a bullet into the man. Looking back with a broad smile, he added, "But not no more."

The leader, who still held his gun, took a step to the side of the strong box and fired at the lock, sending a ricochet singing that made everyone, including his two partners, duck. He bent, pulled off the piece of padlock that remained, and opened the box. "Well, there aren't any gold pieces," he said, "but there looks to be maybe four hundred dollars in bank notes." He looked up at the onion-eater. "Toss me down that mailbag, and then go get the horses the way I said to earlier."

The man threw him the bag, and the boss stuffed the contents of the strong box into it.

He turned to the passengers and said, "All of you line up over there." He nodded toward the train.

Not counting the three outlaws, there had been ten people on board the train when the robbery began. The six still alive lined up as they were told.

"Now, I'm going to go down the line here," the leader said as though he was a school marm speaking to her class, "and I want you to put all of your valuables in this bag. If you do as you're told, you'll all live to tell this horrifying story to your grandkids. If you hold out on me, though, either me or my little friend here—" He jerked his chin at the small man. "—will shoot you dead." He said this with a cordial, ingratiating smile that chilled Billy's blood.

The boss started at the end of the line, taking a watch and a few dollars from the engineer. Next, he came to the older fella, the one Billy had figured to be too drunk to play cribbage. With a grimace, the man reached inside his shirt and unbuckled a thin money belt.

"Here, give me that," said the boss. He peeled open the belt, which contained less than twenty dollars. "I figured an old coot like you'd have a scrawny poke."

He moved on to the well-dressed man and said in a cold, even voice, "Hand it over, mister." The man reached in his jacket pocket and took out a wallet. The leader opened it, pulled out what looked to Billy to be about fifty dollars, and tossed it in his bag.

"Now the watch and ring." The fancy-dressed man stripped off a ring that bore a small red stone and unhooked a watch chain from a buttonhole. He pulled the watch from his vest pocket, and dropped both the ring and watch into the mailbag.

"That's not all you have."

The man looked surprised and gave a vigorous nod. "Why, yes," he said, "yes, sir, it is."

The boss offered a stony look and shoved his hands down into all the pockets of the man's suit coat. He seemed less than satisfied at finding nothing and searched the pockets again. He finally gave up and moved on to Billy. "How 'bout you, kid?" he asked. "Got any of your cribbage winnings?" Billy emptied his pockets into the bag. The man then held the bag out to Frank, and Frank did the same.

The young woman's expression was still blank, and when the boss got to her, he reached down and pulled the wedding ring from her finger. The fight she had shown earlier was gone. She didn't seem to realize the man was in front of her.

The leader dropped the ring into the bag. He closed the bag and latched the clasp on top.

"Did you boys clean these pilgrims out?" asked the onion-eater as he rode up on horseback. He held the reins of two other horses.

"Why, I do believe we have," said the small man.

The leader tied the mailbag to his saddle, took his reins, and climbed up.

"We ain't leavin' yet, are we?" the small man whined when the onion-eater handed over the reins to the small man's horse. "I was plannin' on gettin' me some of this." He walked over to the girl, put his hand on her breast, and squeezed. Frank tensed, but Billy caught his arm before he could do anything foolish.

"We don't have time for that," said the boss.

The small man grinned. "Hell, it won't take long. I promise."

The onion-eater laughed. "Nah, sir. It don't never take him long."

The small man joined the laughter. "It sure don't. I am the

fastest that ever was."

The boss wasn't smiling. "Mount up," he ordered. And Billy could hear something in his voice that apparently the small man could not.

"Hell, boss," he wheedled. "It'd be a shame to waste a pretty 'un like this." He leaned toward the woman and licked her neck.

The boss stood in his stirrups. "Mount up, Goddamn it, and do it now." This time his tone sent the message that everything that had happened up to this point had been one thing; what was to happen next was something else. "We got us a chore to do."

The small man kicked the dirt, but he turned away from the girl and threw a leg over his horse.

"That's better," said the leader. "Sorry I have to do this folks, but there's no other way."

With a casual ease, the leader drew his pistol and shot the fancy-dressed man in the head. A half tick later, the onion-eater and the small man pulled their weapons and began to fire.

The engineer turned to run but was cut down by a shot from the onion-eater. The old drinker was dropped by another shot from the leader.

The small man was the closest to Frank and Billy, and they both charged him at the same time, each going for him from opposite sides of the horse. They grabbed the little man and held on. As they did, he let out a string of curses and tried to fight them off. With all the shooting and the weight of three men on his back, the small man's horse let out a scream and reared. When the horse came up, Frank and Billy were able to roll the man off the horse's rump, and they all three went crashing into the dirt.

Billy had the wind knocked out of him when they landed, and everything seemed to get fuzzy. He shook his head to clear it, and his vision sharpened in time to see the little man level his gun at Billy's face.

"No-o-o-o," Frank screamed. Frank had been thrown to the man's side, and the second before the man pulled the trigger, Frank leapt for his arm. He grabbed it, gave a jerk, and the shot meant for Billy went wide. Frank wrestled the man for the pistol, and Billy pushed himself to his feet. As Billy came up to help his brother, a gush of red exploded from Frank's neck. Frank's body wrenched and spun, and he dropped in a heap across the small man's chest.

Billy's first thought was Frank had been shot by the small man who now struggled beneath the weight of Frank's body, but he realized the angle was wrong. He turned to see the leader sitting astride his horse, staring down at him, his lips peeled into a grin.

The man lifted his gun, and as he did, Billy ducked, spun, and plunged behind the small man's horse. The terrified horse was dancing around, and as Billy put the animal between him and the robbers, he heard the whomp, whomp, whomp of three bullets hitting the horse in the side. The men had fired at Billy at the same time, and all three had hit the horse.

The animal screamed and reared again, but when he came down this time, rather than land on his feet, he crumpled. In one quick move, Billy pulled the small man's long gun from the saddle scabbard and levered a round into the chamber. Another bullet split the air just above his head, and Billy looked up to see the onion-eater riding toward him shooting. Billy brought the rifle to his shoulder and fired. The man was knocked backward out of the saddle, his left foot catching in the stirrup and tearing his boot off.

Billy saw the leader cock his hammer for another shot, but before the man could pull the trigger, Billy, without aiming, fired in the man's direction. Billy's shot missed, but it caused the man to duck, which gave Billy time to drop down low behind the dead horse.

As he did, he saw the small man untangle himself from Frank's body and clamber to his feet. He made a diving leap for the onion-eater's horse, which was between him and Billy. He mounted from the right and wheeled the horse around. Laying low across the saddle, he gave the horse a kick.

Billy came up to put the man in his sights, but he was forced down again when the leader, who was riding off to Billy's left, provided cover for the small man with two quick shots. One shot came within three inches of Billy's head, knocking a chunk of blood and hair out of the dead horse's neck.

By now, the small man was far enough away he provided no target, but Billy thought he still had a shot at the leader. As he laid his front sight into the middle of the man's back, another bullet creased the horse's hide. This shot came from the onion-eater, who lay on his back twenty feet away. The man's chest was covered in gore, but he smiled as he brought the Iver Johnson up.

As the gun came level for another try, Billy swung around and blew off the side of his face. Meat, teeth, and tobacco juice sprayed into the dirt. The hammerless dropped to the ground.

Once he was certain the onion-eater was dead, Billy came to one knee and shouldered the rifle. Both the leader and the small man were riding together, slapping reins in a gallop off to the east. Billy put his sights on the leader and fired, but the man didn't drop.

Billy knew they were too far away and moving too fast for him to hit anything, but he didn't care. Up to then, he'd been operating by instinct. Now, though, he felt a fury take hold and he heard himself scream a wild, crazy-man's scream.

Despite the distance, Billy levered another round and pulled the trigger again.

CHAPTER TWO

When the killers were out of sight, Billy dropped the rifle into the dirt and staggered toward his brother. Even from ten feet away, Billy could see the truth. He went to him, knelt, and put a hand on his shoulder. He leaned forward, and with an easy touch, closed Frank's clouded eyes.

As he did that, a pain sliced through him, and he heaved forward and grabbed his stomach. He clenched his eyes against the force of it. It was a pain that came from grief and rage, but it was physical and as real as a blow from an ax. He gasped but couldn't draw a breath. It was as if all the air had been sucked out of the world.

After a bit the worst seemed to pass, but the memory of it, like a wound, was there, and Billy knew it was a pain that would stay. It was as though something necessary had been carved out of him. Some vital part of him was gone. At first, he fought to throw a rope around the feeling, to tie it down—to understand it—but it was a slippery thing, and he had to give it up.

With shaky, unsteady legs, he pushed himself to his feet. He took his sleeve and wiped the sweat from his forehead. It didn't matter what the feeling was, anyway. And even if it did matter, he would figure it out later, on another day, during some other lifetime, maybe, when there was not so much to do.

There was a sharp sound to Billy's right, and as he spun around, he slapped the leather of his empty holster. His Colt was the first thing the robbers had taken.

Billy's eyes darted around the grisly scene. His first thought was the two men had returned, but he could see no movement. He backed over to the onion-eater's body and grabbed his pistol. He held the weapon in front of him as he moved in the direction of the sound.

He heard it again, and this time he realized it was a groan, and it came from the engineer. Billy holstered the six-gun and ran to kneel beside the man. There was a deep crease along his left temple. Billy rolled him over and saw that bright red covered the side of the man's face. Billy wasn't wearing a bandana, but the engineer was, so Billy pulled it over the man's head and used it to cover the wound.

It took a moment for the man's eyes to focus, but when they did, they locked on Billy and he asked in a raspy voice, "Did you kill 'em?"

"Only one. The other two got away. You've been hit, but you were lucky." *Damned* lucky, Billy thought, although he didn't say that part out loud.

The man lifted his hand and touched his wound. "Funny," he said, "it don't hardly hurt. You'd think a furrow like that along a fella's head would hurt, wouldn't you?" The wonder of it caused his thick eyebrows to knit together. "But it don't, not really."

"Maybe it doesn't now," Billy allowed, "but I'd guess it will before long." He glanced down the track at the locomotive. "Do you think you could get us into Casper?"

"I reckon I could, s'long as you can stoke the firebox."

"Good," Billy said, standing. "You rest here while I—" He looked at the bodies scattered around. "—clean things up."

From the corner of his eye, Billy caught a glimpse of movement between two of the rail cars. He pulled the onion-eater's shooter and called, "All right, I see you there. If you come out with your hands in the air, you won't die." Even as he said the words, he knew it was a lie. If either one of those two killers stepped from between those cars, hands in the air or not, Billy was going to kill him. He would not think twice about it, and he would do it with pleasure.

No one answered, and with caution, Billy edged over to the cars. In a quick move, he rounded the corner and shoved the Iver Johnson into the face of the young woman whose husband had been murdered. She was sitting upright on the ground with her knees against her chest. Her hands were balled into tiny fists at her sides. She was unhurt, but she still wore the same blank expression she'd had earlier.

"Ma'am," Billy said, holstering the gun, "you're all right." He could hear the surprise in his voice. What he meant was she wasn't wounded or dead, but one look told him she was not all right. If possible, her eyes were even emptier than they had been before.

He leaned over so his face was level with hers. "We need to be getting out of here," he said. "Those fellas may be back." The woman didn't respond. "Do you think you can walk?" Billy hoped she could. His legs were still shaky enough he wondered if he could lift her. Then he considered all the bodies he was going to have to load into the boxcar and figured one more wouldn't matter. "If you can't walk," he said, "I'd be glad to carry you."

Still she didn't answer, but when he gave her arm a little tug, she rose to her feet. Her expression didn't change, but she looked at him and allowed him to lead her into the passenger car.

"There you go, ma'am," he said as he sat her in a seat by a window. She aimed her vacant eyes across the dry prairie toward the river—or perhaps it was not the river she was looking at but the horizon beyond, or maybe it wasn't even the horizon, but someplace farther away still. Billy couldn't know, but he did know that, even though she had escaped being shot, she had not avoided injury.

He turned to leave so he could begin his gruesome chores.

"What is your name?" the woman asked before he got to the door.

Her voice was soft, but Billy heard her and came back to where she sat. He took off his hat and said, "Billy Young, ma'am."

She did not face him but continued to gaze out the window. "You killed one of them," she said.

"Yes, ma'am, I did."

"They got what they came for," she said. "What kind of men would do what they did after they had already gotten what they came for?"

Billy gave the woman's question some thought and decided there was only one answer. "They're the kind of men who don't deserve to live," he said in a low, even tone. The boiling rage he had felt earlier when he was taking his futile shots at the fleeing outlaws was still there—and it would stay there, he knew that— but the boil had settled to a simmer.

Now the woman turned to face him, and for the first time tears budded in her dark eyes. "You're right," she agreed, "they don't deserve to live, do they?"

Billy nodded. "And I guarantee you, ma'am, they'll not be alive much longer." He squared his Stetson and turned for the door.

When Casper came into view, Billy had the firebox roaring, and Felix held the locomotive's throttle wide.

"Looks like we're gonna make it," Felix said, but it was a good thing they didn't have to travel any farther. Felix's wound still bled, and the man's face was ashen.

Billy looked out across the prairie toward his hometown. He knew its every street and alley. He had roamed the banks of the

North Platte River that ran through its center. He'd explored just about every crag and cranny of the big, asymmetrical, broad-shouldered mountain that rose behind the town to the south. He had fished from the rotting dock once used by the Mormons for their river ferry and played with Frank in the old, deserted fort. This was a familiar place.

But now it all looked different.

Felix pulled into the station. He brought the train to a stop, gave Billy a weak smile, and slid down to his bench.

"You rest here," Billy said. "I'll make sure you get some help."

No one paid much attention as Billy swung out of the locomotive's cab, but after he walked down the line and opened the door to the boxcar that held the bodies, a crowd began to form.

"My God, Billy," asked an old man, cupping his hand over his nose to block out the smell of death. "What happened here?"

Billy ignored the man's question. "Find the doctor," he said. "Felix, the engineer, is up in the locomotive yonder, and he's been shot." Billy began to scan the crowd for Orozco Valdez, his and Frank's friend and hired man. He was to come into town that day for supplies, meet Frank and Billy at the station, and drive them home. "I reckon Felix'll be all right," Billy added, "but find his son, anyhow, and bring the boy around. My guess is Felix'd like to see him." He jerked his head toward the passenger car. "There's a woman in there the doc'll need to take a look at as well."

He turned toward the window, and the young woman was still there, staring at that distant place. He touched the brim of his hat, but if she noticed him, he couldn't tell. Her face never changed expression.

Billy looked out over the crowd and caught a glimpse of Orozco waving from the seat of a buckboard he had parked in the alley. Pushing through the jumble of people, Billy made his way toward the man.

"I'm sure Hugo Dorling's gonna wanna talk to you about all this, Billy," the old geezer shouted after him. Hugo Dorling was the Deputy U.S. Marshal and the closest thing to law they had in the area. A man named Dale Jarrell was the county sheriff, but everyone agreed Jarrell was pretty much worthless and would be looking for new employment after the next election. "Last I heard," the old man added, "Hugo's over to Lander, but he's supposed to be back later today."

"I'll be easy to find," Billy said.

The Mexican hopped down from the wagon when he saw Billy approaching. "Billy," he called with a smile, "where have you been? The train is late." He extended his large hand, and Billy gave it a shake. Orozco was the strongest man Billy had ever known, and his hand was thick with callous and muscle. Orozco glanced at the crowd that had formed in front of the boxcar. "And what is all the commotion?" he asked.

Billy nodded to the edge of a large watering trough. "Sit down there, Rosco," he said, "on the edge of that trough. I have some disturbing news."

Billy had known Orozco for years, but that didn't make the chore any easier. Orozco first came to work for Joshua Young, Frank and Billy's father, before the boys were big enough to sit a horse. Until then he'd traveled the West working many jobs, but he and Josh became friends fast, and the young Mexican decided this time he wanted to put down roots.

Billy cleared his throat, and with little detail he related the events of the robbery.

When he finished, Orozco lowered his head and stared at his powerful hands. "I am sorry for Frank, Billy," he said. Lifting his eyes, he added, "It is a hateful thing. It is a hard thing to hear."

Billy gave his friend's shoulder a squeeze and said, "Find

some blankets or something to wrap Frank in and get him loaded onto the buckboard. I'll be back." With that, he turned on his boot heel and walked away.

"Wait, where are you going?" Orozco called. Billy heard the man, but he didn't answer. All of his life Billy had been a talker. Now, he discovered he had no patience with words. He left the train yard, passed through the station, and walked the couple of blocks to the Portrait Studio of Elmo T. Bickel. Billy stepped through the door, and a tiny bell above his head jingled.

As Billy closed the door, a tall, skeletal man stepped through a set of dark draperies that separated the front area of the studio from the back. The place was filled with strange chemical smells, and when the man entered the room, the odors grew stronger. The smells swarmed about him like bees.

"Yes, sir," he said, "may I help you?" The proprietor wore a white shirt with a high, tight collar. Dark sleeve-protectors covered his forearms, and around his bald skull he wore a Celluloid visor.

"I need you to use your photography, Mr. Bickel, to make me a picture," Billy said. "And I need it right away."

"Why of course, young man. Would this be a portrait of you or your family, perhaps?"

"No," Billy said, "it would not. Also, we'll not be making the photograph here. I need you to take it at the depot."

Elmo Bickel's face was devoid of hair, including eyebrows, but the two patches of parchment-colored skin above his eyes rose more than an inch. "At the depot?" he asked.

"That's right. Can you do that?"

"Yes," Mr. Bickel answered. "Yes, I can. Although I will have to charge you for the expense of—"

Billy interrupted. "Charge what you will. I don't care about that, but I want it done now. Once the photograph is made, how soon can I get the picture?"

"Well, of course you must realize in the science of photography there are a number of processes a practitioner needs to perform. I would have to—"

Billy leaned over the counter and fixed the man with a hard stare.

Mr. Bickel swallowed. "I could have it for you by tomorrow morning, I s'pose. I couldn't have it any sooner."

"The morning will be fine," Billy said. "Grab your gear. I'll help you carry it."

By the time Billy and the photographer arrived at the station, the doctor had come and gone, taking both Felix and the young woman with him. Orozco had removed Frank from the train, wrapped him in a sheet of canvas, and placed him in the buckboard.

The undertaker, a fat man who always seemed to sweat, had his hearse backed up to the boxcar and was unloading the rest of the bodies.

Billy shoved his head into the boxcar's open door. Through the dusty gloom, he could barely see the large undertaker tending to his duties, but he could hear his heavy breathing well enough. The undertaker's name was Barnett Teasdale, and from what Billy could tell, the man was sweating more than ever.

Billy looked at the body the undertaker was carrying and saw it was the fancy-dressed man. "I'm looking for the robber," Billy said. The fat man's jowls bounced as he nodded toward the hearse. Billy turned and saw the onion-eater had already been loaded.

"This won't take long, Mr. Teasdale," Billy said, and he reached in and took hold of the dead man's ankles. He gave the body a jerk and pulled it from the hearse. The crowd of onlookers gasped when the back of the man's head hit the depot's masonry pavement.

"See here, young man," the undertaker scolded. "You show

some respect for the dead."

Billy paid the man no mind. "Where do you want him, Mr. Bickel?" Billy asked the photographer.

The tall, thin man appeared stunned. "D-d-do you mean to say you want me to photograph a d-d-dead man?" Bickel asked. It seemed the photographer had developed a stutter.

"That is just what I mean," Billy said.

The photographer glanced over his shoulder at the baffled crowd who stood and watched. He dug an index finger into his stiff collar and pulled it away from his neck. Looking up, he squinted at the late afternoon sky. "He needs to have the sun on him," the man said. "So I reckon where he is'll do, but he can't be on the ground like that." The man opened a huge mahogany tripod. "He needs to be higher so I can get a straight-on shot."

Billy gave a curt nod and crossed to Orozco's buckboard. He took a hemp rope from the back and returned to the body. He made a loop and curled it under the dead man's arms, dragged him closer to the boxcar, and ran the end of the rope through the top rung of a steel ladder that rose from the bottom of the car to the roof. Billy then hoisted the dead body halfway up the ladder and tied off the rope. "There you go," he said.

The incredulous photographer stared at Billy, turned, and glanced again at the open-mouthed faces of the crowd.

"I-I just have to finish assembling my equipment," he said, and he began to scamper about.

As Bickel set up, Billy tore a strip of cloth from the tail of the dead man's shirt and used that to tie the man's head back against the ladder. He tried to situate the head in profile so the gaping hole on the lower right-hand portion of the man's face wouldn't show, but the hole was large enough that it was difficult to hide.

When Billy was finished, he turned to the photographer and asked, "Are you ready?"

"Y-yes," said the photographer.

"Good," Billy said. "Go ahead."

As Billy stepped away from the boxcar, he heard someone in the crowd mutter, "I believe Billy Young has done gone stark-ravin' crazy."

CHAPTER THREE

When Orozco and Billy pulled the buckboard into the ranch-house yard, Billy said, "We'll unload the supplies then get some picks and shovels and head down to the Plot." The Plot was what they called the small family cemetery. It was located near a stream a little over a mile from the house. There was a nice view of the mountain to the south and the old fort and the town of Casper to the northwest. Beyond the town was the wide, expansive prairie. Frank and Billy had often joked—at least they had until their father's death—of how such beautiful vistas were wasted on the folks who inhabited the Plot.

"But, Billy," Orozco said, "don't you think we should wait to do this? The neighbors, your friends, they will want to pay their respects."

"We'll bury him tonight," Billy said as he jumped from the buckboard. "Start unloading the supplies. I'll fetch the tools."

At first they took turns with the digging, but after a bit, and over Orozco's protests, Billy finished the job himself. The exertion relaxed him some. Besides, he wanted to dig his brother's grave alone.

Once Billy patted the last spadeful of earth onto the grave, he picked up the tools and headed toward the buckboard.

Orozco didn't follow. "Billy," he said, "we should not leave without saying words over the grave."

"There aren't any words that'd change what happened." Billy dropped the picks and shovels into the back of the wagon and climbed onto the seat. "Let's get going."

Orozco leveled Billy a disgusted look, turned back to the grave and began to pray. Billy watched and waited. After a while, Orozco crossed himself and walked to the wagon.

Billy looked down at the older man. "I'm sorry, Rosco. I never meant to stop your prayers. Hell, I knew I couldn't even if I wanted to. I just meant I'd not be a part of it."

Orozco offered Billy the same patient expression Billy had often seen as he and Frank grew up. The Mexican climbed onto the wagon and dropped to the seat. "No matter what you meant, I prayed just now," he advised, "and I will pray some more, and you *will* be a part of it whether you wish to be or not."

Billy didn't respond. He knew the man took his Roman beliefs to heart. Billy gave the reins a snap, and he and Orozco drove to the ranch house in silence.

When they arrived, Hugo Dorling, the Deputy U.S. Marshal, was sitting on the Youngs' front porch smoking a cigarette.

"Evenin', Billy," Dorling said, coming to his feet as they drove up. He looked to the Mexican. "Rosco."

Orozco nodded to the deputy and took the reins from Billy. Billy climbed down, and Orozco drove the rig to the barn.

"Sorry to hear about what happened," said Dorling, taking a draw from his smoke.

Billy mounted the porch steps, and as he passed the deputy, he said, "I'm having a whiskey. Care to join me?"

"Why, I'd like that fine." Dorling crushed the cigarette butt with the toe of his boot, kicked it into the yard, and followed Billy into the house.

Hugo Dorling was a man of forty, with the hard, angular, weather-beaten looks of the cowboy and range detective he once had been. It was said that in earlier days, before there was any law other than what people made for themselves, Hugo Dorling had brought more wrong-doers to justice than any other man around. Billy remembered when the topic came up of Hugo's "justice," people mentioned it with a wink and a smile.

Billy had taken off his gun belt when he was digging the grave, and had it draped across his shoulder. Once they were inside, he went through the parlor to the gun cabinet. His father felt a gun was not worth anything if it couldn't be gotten to, so ever since Frank and Billy had been old enough not to shoot themselves, the key to the cabinet had been left in its lock, which was where it was now and where it had been for years.

Billy opened the cabinet's door and dropped in the holster, which still held the onion-eater's pistol. Although the Iver Johnson was in fair condition, it was a cheaply made weapon and a poor trade for Billy's own pearl-gripped forty-five that had been pulled from his hip by the leader. Tomorrow he'd refill the holster with one of the Colts from the cabinet. Leaving the key in the lock, he closed the door.

Hugo, who'd been watching, followed Billy into the kitchen where Billy pumped water into a basin. Once he'd washed, he pulled a bottle of Scotland whiskey from a cupboard and poured a couple of stiff drinks.

Dorling seated himself at the eating table in the center of the room, and when Billy placed the glass of whiskey in front of him, Dorling lifted it toward the younger man. "To your good brother, Frank, and the fine men who died today beside the railroad tracks," and he tossed back three-quarters of what Billy had poured. Billy nodded and took a sip from his own glass. He was an inexperienced drinker and incapable of throwing the whiskey against the back of his throat the way the deputy had done.

"Dale Jarrell gathered a posse after you left town this afternoon, and they rode out to the spot where the robbery and murders took place. I guess they tried to track the two bastards you didn't kill, but they didn't have no luck. Jarrell's a damned fool, but he had a couple of good men with him who told me the bandits went into the river, and the posse couldn't pick up their trail again after that."

"And that's as much as Jarrell will ever do," Billy said.

"I expect you're right," agreed Dorling. "He made a show of it today, but he won't take it any further. That's just his way."

"How 'bout you?" Billy asked.

Dorling reached into his vest pocket and pulled out his makings. He peeled off a paper, shook in a line of tobacco, and, with one hand, twisted it into a cigarette.

It was amazing to watch the ease with which he performed the task, but Billy knew this was a man who could roll a smoke in a raging Wyoming wind while straddling a surly horse. It was no challenge to do it sitting at the Youngs' kitchen table.

The deputy ran the head of a wooden match against the underside of the table. It popped into flame, and he lit his cigarette. "Well," he began, "workin' for the United States of America the way I do, as a rule, robbery and murder wouldn't be in my jurisdiction, but one of the things these fellas stole is a postal mailbag, and that puts 'er right in my bailiwick." He blew a stream of gray-blue smoke at the ceiling.

"Does that mean you'll be going after them, Hugo?" Billy asked.

"That's one of the reasons I rode out, Billy. I'll be lookin' into it, but I can't do it right away."

"What do you mean you can't do it right away?"

"I spent the last two days over in Lander. Late last week, our Indian Agent—apparently the son of some congressman from back East—was here in Casper on business and got his throat slit out in the alley behind the Wentworth Hotel."

"What does that have to do with you? You just said murder wasn't in your jurisdiction."

"Well, the rules seem to change when the fella who's been murdered is a federal agent, not to mention the son of a congressman." Dorling rested his left ankle on his right knee and tipped the ash that had formed on the end of his cigarette into the cuff of his jeans. "And another thing, the knife used as the murder weapon was found in the alley, and it's clearly Arapaho. Some folks figure a couple of young bucks off the Reservation followed him here and killed 'im. That's what I was doin' over in Lander, snoopin' around on the Res."

Billy had always liked Hugo Dorling. When they were boys, he and Frank would sit on the kitchen floor playing cribbage and listening to the conversations of Hugo and their father as they sat at this very table sharing a whiskey.

"I got a telegram today," Dorling went on to say, "and the United States Marshal hisself is on his way up from Cheyenne." He glanced at the Regulator clock hanging on the wall behind Billy. "My guess is he'll be in town by the time I get back. I can't remember the last time that son of a bitch bothered to come all the way up to Casper." He gave a smirk and took a pull from his cigarette. He let the smoke out as he spoke. "Of course, in his defense, it's hard to travel very far with your head stuck up a federal judge's ass." Hugo was a man quick to laugh at his own jokes, but he didn't laugh at that one. "Anyhow, the point is, I'd like to chase down your brother's killers, but for a while, this Indian Agent thing'll take priority over everythin' else, includin' mail robberies and the murders of local citizens."

Billy shrugged and took a sip of his whiskey. In truth, he didn't care one way or the other about any of this. It had nothing to do with him.

Hugo cleared his throat. "Folks back in town mentioned your behavior this afternoon was a little peculiar, Billy, and they're worried. They like you, and they're afraid you might do somethin' foolish."

"Like what?"

"Like maybe tryin' to find those two fellas yourself."

"If that's what they think," Billy said, "they're right. That's just what I aim to do. Those fellas'll be dead shortly after the next time I see 'em."

Dorling blinked twice in apparent disbelief. He then laughed out loud. "Good God, boy," he said as he finished off the last of his drink, "you could at least show some guile. After all, I am an officer of the damned law, you know."

Billy lifted the bottle and poured another finger of whiskey into the man's glass. "It was good of you to come out here, Hugo, to explain your situation and the worries of the town, but it doesn't matter to me one way or the other whether you or Jarrell or anyone else goes after those two men. You can do it or not do it as you see fit. But I'll make no secret of the fact that I will be going after them, and when I find them, I'll kill them. Whatever happens after that, happens."

"I can understand what you're sayin', Billy, and I don't blame you. And, if you do kill 'em, I expect there ain't a jury around here that'd find you guilty. Things're different than when I was a younger man, but they ain't so different yet, thank the Lord, that folks'd punish a grievin' brother for seekin' justice from a pair like that. No, that ain't the problem. These fellas are a couple of very bad men. I talked to Felix before I rode out, and he said he'd never seen a man more cold-blooded than the little one, nor a faster or truer shot than the one who was the leader. Felix told me how that fella killed the two trainmen who were runnin' for their lives—" He snapped his fingers. "—just that damned fast. It's clear to me a man who can do that is an accomplished gunman, and you are barely more than a boy. What's more, you're a rancher, not a shooter. I expect these sons of bitches'd make short work of you, Billy, and my advice is to leave 'em alone. Either me or some other lawman'll get 'em sooner or later, if not for this crime then for their next. We always do. It ain't common for men of that sort to get old and die in their beds." He jabbed a thick finger in Billy's direction to emphasize what he was saying. "This ain't a job for you, son. It truly ain't."

"I appreciate that, Hugo."

"You appreciate it, but you're gonna go ahead just the same. Am I right?"

When Billy didn't answer, the older man laughed again, softer this time and without much humor. "Well, Billy-boy," he said, tossing off his drink as he stood, "I don't guess I expected anything else, but I had to protect my own conscience by ridin' out and havin' my say." He turned for the door, and Billy followed. "My guess is those fellas're long gone. I hope so, anyhow. I know you want your revenge, and I know you deserve to have it, too, but just the same, for your sake, I hope them fellas're gone."

Once they were outside, the deputy took his reins from around the porch rail and climbed atop his roan. "I reckon I know how you feel, though, boy. If I was your age, I'd do the same." He gave a shrug. "Hell," he added, "I'm better than twenty years older than you and I'd do the same still." He flicked what was left of his cigarette into the dirt. "But you be careful."

"I will, sir."

Hugo seemed to give that some thought, and with the hint of a frown, he found Billy's eyes and locked his own eyes onto them. "I doubt you will when it comes down to it, but you need to bear in mind, Billy Young, that these two fellas are the kind who kill for sport."

Giving a quick little wave, Hugo wheeled his horse toward the gate.

CHAPTER FOUR

The next morning Billy went straight to Elmo Bickel's portrait shop. "I'm here for my photograph of the killer," Billy said when Bickel came through the draperies.

The skinny man seemed uncomfortable. He nodded and disappeared again behind the curtains. He was gone a few seconds and returned carrying the picture.

Billy took it and held it toward the light. The photographic print was four inches by six inches and showed the onion-eater from the waist up. Although it clearly revealed there was a chunk missing from the lower right-hand side of the man's face, it was still a good likeness and what Billy wanted. "This'll do fine, Mr. Bickel," Billy said. "What do I owe you?"

The man swallowed and said, "T-t-ten dollars."

Billy felt himself blink. Ten dollars seemed a little steep for using a machine to produce the image of a corpse, but he dug into his pocket and placed the money on the man's counter.

As he turned toward the door to leave, Bickel said, "I want you to know, young fella, it ain't my practice to photograph dead men."

"Why's that?" Billy asked, turning back to face the man.

The photographer seemed surprised at such a question. "Because it ain't seemly. That's why."

"Well, then, Mr. Bickel, I reckon every time I kill a fella in the future, I'll have to take my photography business elsewhere."

Bickel came around the counter. "You're a smart-aleck, Billy

Young. I'm sorry 'bout what happened to your brother, but that don't give you the right to sass your elders. Besides, what kind of a fella'd want to carry around a picture of a man he'd killed, anyhow? It ain't right. It's downright sick, if you ask me."

The rage Billy felt the day before still simmered, and the ranting of this skinny man's squeaky voice was raising it again to a boil. Billy took a step forward. When he did, Bickel scurried back around his counter. Billy opened his mouth to say something. He wasn't sure what it was going to be, but he was certain it would not be kind. He stopped himself, though, before those words erupted, and instead he touched the brim of his hat and said, "You have a pleasant morning, Mr. Bickel. And thank you again for the fine work. I appreciate it."

With that he turned and left the shop.

Billy felt his heart racing. There was no reason to get mad at anything a fool like Bickel had to say. Billy knew he had to keep a tight rein on himself if he was going to accomplish what had to be done.

He stepped off the boardwalk and crossed to the hitching post where he'd tied Badger, the four-year-old gray Billy most often rode. Frank had named the horse when he was a colt because in those days the gray was about as mean as a cornered badger. He was still feisty but had mellowed some since.

Billy took another look at the photograph of the onion-eater. He had to admit the man was a grisly sight, but despite that—or perhaps because of it—the look of the dead man made Billy feel a bit better.

He glanced again at the picture and then tucked it into a saddle bag. Billy would not rest until he saw the other two killers in the same condition.

That thought made him feel better still. He wasn't positive that what he planned to do would pay off, but at least he was doing something.

He swung himself onto Badger's back and headed for the west side of Center Street.

That part of Center was the area of Casper that catered to the tastes of rough men. Since he remembered the killers had boarded the train back down the line, Billy doubted they lived in Casper, but he also knew if they had been around these parts very long at all, they'd spent some time—and perhaps lots of it—in the pool rooms, saloons, and whorehouses located on the west side of Center. It was his hope to learn the names of the onion-eater and, with luck, his two companions, and it seemed to Billy that Center was the most likely spot to begin his search.

He visited a dozen low places on that first day. He showed his photograph to a couple of dozen bartenders and working girls without any luck, until late in the afternoon when he came upon The Westerner. It was a seedy establishment even by the rough standards of the area. The place needed a coat of paint, and even more, a good fumigation. It smelled of stale tobacco smoke, spilled alcohol, and a few other things Billy made no attempt to identify.

It was still early, and the saloon was empty except for a man behind the bar and a fat woman who sat at a table next to a window. She held what appeared to be a dime novel and glanced Billy's way only for a second before she went back to her reading.

The bartender was a foppish-looking fella with thin, slick hair he combed down over his forehead. He had a tiny, well-scissored mustache that marked the line of his upper lip, and he wore a bright blue shirt with a large collar and puffy sleeves. Billy came to the bar, and the man greeted him with a smile that showed a mouthful of dingy teeth. "Afternoon, mister," he said. "What's your poison?" Billy suspected the bartender had offered this clever welcome many times in the past.

During the course of the day, Billy had learned that the

residents along this side of Center were wary of strange men asking questions, so he returned the smile in the hopes of setting aside the man's caution before it could begin.

"I wouldn't care for anything to drink," Billy said. "I'd just like to visit with you for a bit, if I could."

"Well, sir—" the bartender's own smile broadened. "—I expect that'd be possible. What's on your mind?" He leaned his forearms on the edge of the bar, and Billy stuck the picture in his hand. "What d'ya have here?" the fella asked, his smile still wide. After he'd had a look at what he held, his voice rose an octave when he said, "My God, this man is dead."

Out of the corner of his eye, Billy saw the fat lady's head pop up. "Yes, sir," he agreed, "that's a fact. He's as dead as any man can be."

The bartender dropped the photograph onto the bar as though he was afraid some of the gore that covered the dead man's shirt might come off on his fingers. Looking across at Billy, he asked, "What's this all about?" His smile was gone.

Billy tapped the onion-eater's grisly face. "You ever seen that fella?"

"What?"

"Do you recall this man ever coming into your barroom here? He might've been with a couple of other men. One is small, no bigger than this." Billy stuck his hand out five feet above the floor. "The other one's about my size, maybe a little bigger. He wears a black leather vest and keeps his holster low on the right, tied with a leather thong to his thigh."

The man gave his head a fast shake. "No, I've never seen him. Never saw this fella nor his friends neither one."

"Slow down," Billy said. "Take another look. I need to locate this dead man's two companions. It's important."

"Why do you want to find 'em?" the bartender asked.

Billy offered the fella another smile, but this time it wasn't as warm as the one he'd given earlier. This time the smile was as cold as December.

It was clear the bartender felt the chill because his gaze dropped, and he lifted the picture. He held it by the edges and gave it another look, a longer look than he had before. After a bit, he shook his head again and repeated, "No, I ain't never seen him. I'm sure of it." He handed the photograph back to Billy and jerked a thumb toward the window. "Try Agnes over yonder," he suggested. "Maybe she has." He seemed eager for Billy to move along.

"Thanks for your time," Billy said and crossed to the woman at the table.

Before he had a chance to open his mouth, the big woman said, "Name's Agnes, cowboy. Pull up a chair."

Billy figured her weight to be better than three hundred pounds. Coiled atop her head in swirly loops and spirals was what looked to be an additional twenty pounds of coal-black hair. Two long tresses of it dangled in front of her large ears. She had tiny dark eyes, which were set into the flesh of her face like raisins in a bun. Her jowls were rouged and her thin lips were painted. She wore a gauzy pink dress with straps that were lost in the meat of her round, white shoulders. Leaning forward, she pushed against the edge of the table, causing her melon-sized breasts to bulge and threaten the stitching of her bodice.

Billy thanked her for the invitation to sit, scooted out a chair, and dropped himself into it. He tried not to stare but he was fighting a losing battle. Billy recognized his experience was limited, but there was more creamy pink flesh on the other side of this table than he, until now, figured was possible to hang on a human skeleton.

She gave him a smile, showing white, straight teeth. Two small lines creased the space between her penciled eyebrows, but apart from those two lines, her face was smooth. It was a face Billy thought might have been pretty, even beautiful, a couple of hundred pounds ago.

"What's your business, young buck?" the fat woman asked. "You of a mind for a little frolic?" Her eyebrows rose, and she lifted her pudgy hands to the material covering her breasts. She pulled the already low-cut neckline down farther, exposing eight inches of cleavage and the hint of two light brown nipples.

Billy sat straight up and said in a voice he knew was too loud the second the words leapt out, "No, no, ma'am. I don't . . . I mean, I do, I guess, but I . . ."

The big woman slapped the table and bellowed a roaring laugh. She pulled the top of her dress back up and said, "Let me see your picture there, fella. I know just about every man in town." She gave Billy a wink. "Most of them I know real well."

Billy placed the photograph on the table and Agnes scooped it up, pushing aside the book she'd been reading as she did. Billy had read a few dime novels himself, but he had never seen this one. It was by some fella named James. Billy cocked his head for a better look at the title. *Daisy Miller.* It looked like a book for a woman, Billy observed.

"I've seen him," Agnes said after a bit. And when she said it, Billy's mouth went dry. "Of course," she added, "as I recall, his right jaw was a little larger when I saw him than it appears to be in this photo." She and Billy shared a quick smile. "But he wasn't any better looking then than he is right here."

"What's his name? Do you know his name?"

Agnes dropped the picture to the table. "Never heard it," she said. "I guess it was maybe two or three weeks ago he was in."

"Was he with anyone?" Billy asked.

She nodded. "Yep." She jabbed the white sausage of her index finger in the direction of the bartender. "He was with a little fella like the one you described to Carl. It's the little one I remember most." She took her eyes off Billy and said as much to herself as to him, "He was mean, that one was. Crazy mean."

That pretty much described the little man, all right, but Billy asked why she said it just the same.

"Because I've seen mean before," Agnes answered. "And I've seen crazy. And I can recognize 'em both."

Before Billy could think of a response, the woman tapped the picture and said, "This one and the little one were already drunk when they came in. Mostly they were looking for girls, which is fine. That's what we do. They paid their three dollars each and took a couple of my girls out back. They weren't gone more than ten minutes when I heard Betty, the girl who went with the little one, start to scream." Agnes's thin lips became even thinner with the telling of it. "At nights I keep a man named Jacob around for just such times. He's a big one and sometimes shows a streak of mean himself. Well, sir, Jake and I ran into the back, and there was Betty, naked, with blood streaming down the side of her face and neck. I swear, I've never seen so much blood before in my life. Well, the back windows were opened, and the little one and his friend here—" again she tapped the picture "—were gone."

"What'd happened?" Billy asked.

"He'd bit her ear."

"What?" Billy wasn't sure he'd heard the woman right.

"He was doing his business with her, and during the course of it, he bit off most of the girl's right ear." She took her index finger and drew an invisible line across her own jug ear from the arch at the top down past the lobe. "We found it on the floor where he spit it out."

Billy tried to swallow away the cotton that plugged his throat.

"Jake ran out into the alley after them, but by then they were gone."

"Was the other man I mentioned with them?" Billy asked.

"No, it was just those two. The dead fella here and the little one, Jeets."

"Jeets? You know his name?"

She nodded. "Somewhere along the line, I guess, he mentioned it to Betty, but she didn't know if that was his first name or last name. It could be a nickname, I reckon. It's not anything I've ever heard before."

Billy felt the blood pumping in his chest, and he had to stand with the excitement of it. "Did he tell this Betty anything else?"

"Not really, I don't think. He was pretty drunk, and they weren't here long." Her broad brow furrowed as though something was coming to mind. "Wait a minute. Now that you mention it, she did say something else."

"What's that?" Billy sat back down and leaned across the table.

"I guess he was complaining about how tired he was from having to work cattle so hard the week before. Betty figured he was worried about being able to do what he came here for and was fixing it so he had an excuse. That sort of thing happens from time to time."

"So he works on a ranch," Billy said.

"That's what it sounded like."

"Did he say where?"

"No, but I tell you, this Jeets fella was no Prince Charming." She leaned back in her chair and Billy could hear it creak with her weight. "During the course of things, he told Betty instead of coming all the way to Casper, he and his partner should've just gone into Probity because it was closer and the girls there were lots prettier, anyway."

Billy smacked a fist into his palm. "Probity," he said. "That's fine. That's *damned* fine." He pushed himself away from the table, reached down, grabbed Agnes's hand, and began to give it a shake. "Thanks so much, Miss Agnes. You've been a world of help. You really have." Every time he pumped her arm, the flesh above her elbow billowed and rolled. "I can't thank you enough," he said. Scooping up the picture, he dashed for the door.

Agnes, who seemed to enjoy Billy's excitement, laughed and called after him, "You come back, young fella, when you're in the mood for a frolic. I just might give a pretty young cowpoke like yourself a generous discount."

Billy could still hear her laughter as he tossed a leg over the gray.

CHAPTER FIVE

After he left Agnes at The Westerner, Billy returned to the ranch, did his chores before supper, and went to bed early. He rose the next morning at sunrise. Once he was washed and dressed, he fried a couple of eggs and drank a cup of coffee. He then locked the place up and crossed the yard to the bunk house, where Rosco had a room in back. He told the older man he'd be gone for a few days, which meant Rosco would be on his own keeping up with things.

"I'll make it up to you once all this is behind us," he promised and left the room before Rosco could ask any questions.

Billy hurried to the barn, saddled Badger, and aimed the horse's nose east toward Probity, Wyoming.

Probity was a small town also located on the North Platte River downstream from Casper. It was smaller than Casper, and like Casper, it was a town that first got its foothold when the army established a fort in the area during the Indian wars.

It was midafternoon when Billy loped across the river bridge west of town. What he hoped to do was locate someone here in Probity who knew this fella Jeets and where he worked. Once he found and dealt with Jeets, his business would be halfway complete.

The railroad tracks ran north and south just past the bridge going into town, and Billy slowed Badger up as they crossed the rails. Once they were into the Probity business district, he spotted a long funeral procession moving down Main Street. There were a dozen buggies and carriages of various types in the cortege, all led by a fancy hearse with a couple of footmen hanging on the back. A brass band of fifteen musicians played a mournful dirge and brought up the rear.

The sight of the funeral hit a wounded spot in Billy, and he tensed himself against the pain of it.

There's no time for that now. No time.

As the cortege approached, Billy edged Badger to the side of the street and dismounted. A man wearing a pair of overalls and holding the reins to a mule had also stopped for the procession, and they both stood together and watched the mourners pass.

"Who died?" Billy asked. The man had his hat off and was holding it over his chest, so Billy did the same.

Before he answered, the man spit a stream of tobacco juice into the dirt. "A fella name of Caldwell Unger," he said. "They just finished his service up at the Community Church, and now they're hauling him out to the graveyard north of town."

"He must've been an important fella," said Billy. "It looks like quite the funeral."

The man shrugged. "He was a lawyer, if you consider that important. I ain't never had much use for 'em myself, although from what I understand, this Unger was a good enough sort. Smart is what I hear. Intelligent-like, ya know?"

"How'd he die?"

"Shot hisself in the guts."

"You don't say? Damn, that doesn't sound too smart to me."

"Well, it was a hunting accident. They figure he slipped and fell, when he did, his rifle went off and killed him right on the spot."

"Damned hard luck," Billy observed.

"Ain't it, though."

The last of the buggies rolled by, and the man put on his hat and turned toward his mule.

Billy hadn't eaten in better than six hours, and he could feel his stomach grumble. "Before you go, mister, maybe you can tell me if there's a place around where a fella could find a bite to eat."

"There's a couple of 'em. The Glendale House. That's a hotel with a restaurant right up the street here. And there's Lottie's Café a block over on Second Street." He jerked his head to the northeast. "I'd choose Lottie's, if I was you—better food and cheaper to boot, unless you have problems with Lottie being a Louisiana Negress." He swung himself aboard the mule. "That sort of thing don't bother me none—never has—but I know it's a problem for some."

"Well, I'm not sure if it bothers me or not," Billy said. "I never met anyone from Louisiana before."

The man smiled and shot another stream of juice into the street. "You give Lottie a try. She'll fill you up." He nudged his mule and rode away.

Billy found Lottie's easy enough. Before he went in, he loosened the cinch on Badger's saddle and let him drink from the trough out front. He then took out some oats and strapped on the horse's feed bag.

It didn't look like too many folks had a problem with Lottie. The café was crowded and noisy, but Billy located a table toward the back, ordered some ham, butter beans, and cornbread, and ate until he expected he might pop.

A pretty almond-skinned girl of maybe thirteen or fourteen had been waiting on him, but as she came carrying a pot of coffee to refill his cup for the third time, a thin Negro woman stepped out of the back and said, "Fay, honey, you go on and wash up them dishes. I'll take care of the customers for a while." She took the pot from the girl and filled Billy's cup.

"That was a mighty fine meal, ma'am," Billy said. "I think I might need to loosen my belt."

"Why, thank ya, young man. I'm glad ya liked it. I got some mincemeat pie in the back, if you have a sweet tooth." The woman looked to be in her late thirties or early forties and had what sounded to Billy like a kind of distorted French accent mixed in with her thick Southern drawl.

"Oh, no thanks, ma'am. If I ate another bite, I'm not sure my horse'd be able to tote me around." Billy glanced out over the crowd. "Looks like you stay pretty busy in here."

The woman smiled and said, "We do jus' fine. It keeps me and my daughter a-hoppin'. That's for sure. Are you new in town?"

"Just arrived from Casper," Billy said.

"Did you come all the way from Casper jus' for a plate of my butter beans?"

Billy laughed. "No, ma'am, I didn't, although I might the next time you have 'em on the menu. What I'm doing is looking for a fella who lives somewhere around here."

"Oh, who might that be? 'Bout evah-body in town comes in here from time to time."

"He's a little fella with the name of Jeets."

Lottie stiffened. "Is Jeets a friend of yours?" she asked.

"No," said Billy, "he's not a friend. I don't even know his whole name."

"His name is Jeets Duvall. How did a fine-lookin' boy like you ever come to have dealings with the likes of Jeets Duvall?"

"It's a complex story, ma'am. And I reckon whatever future dealings I'll be having with him'll be brief."

Billy heard a bitter sound slide into his voice, and he guessed Lottie had heard it too because her jaw line tightened, and she didn't ask any more questions.

She did offer a warning, however. "You be careful," she said. "He's a bad 'un. He runs with Noah Baxter, and he's a bad 'un, too."

Billy reached inside his shirt and pulled out the photograph. "Would that fella be the Noah Baxter you're referring to, by any chance?"

"Well," Lottie said, her eyes widening, "he don't appear to be at his best right here, but, yes, sir, that's Baxter, all right." She handed the picture back. "I knew anyone strange enough to go 'round eatin' onions like they was derned pomegranates would come to a bad end."

"Did you ever see Jeets and this Baxter fella running with another man? A bigger man. A man who looks like he might have a few more brains than the both of them put together?"

Lottie shook her head. "You're gonna have to narrow your question down a little more'n that. If you're lookin' for a fella who might have more brains than them two, you're talkin' 'bout a whole lotta folks."

"This man's as bad as they are," Billy said, "maybe worse. He carries himself like a man who makes his living with a gun."

"No," Lottie said, "I never seen neither one of them with anyone else. I figured there was never anyone else 'round here low enough to run with 'em."

"Do you have any idea where I could find this Jeets Duvall?"

"Well, sir, for a while there, him and Baxter was doin' mechanic work for the railroad."

"Working for the railroad? I'd heard they were hands on a ranch."

"That could be," said Lottie. "There was some talk they'd been fired from the railroad two, maybe three months ago. No tellin' where they went after that. They could be cowboying, I s'pose. I ain't seen 'em around here, so I was hopin' they'd done left the country. I guess we weren't that lucky, though."

"Do you figure there might be someone with the railroad who'd know where they went?"

"Fritz Gruber's the fella who's in charge of the repair gang. If he ain't out on a job, you could probably find him in the mechanic's shop down past the depot."

Billy stood. "Thank ya, ma'am. I think I'll ride over there right now and visit with this Mr. Gruber."

Lottie frowned. "You sure findin' Jeets Duvall's somethin' you really need to do?" she asked. There was the sound of a mother in her tone.

"I'm sure."

"Well," the woman allowed, shaking her head, "I learned a long time ago that you can't talk *any* man outta very much once his mind's made up, and you can't talk a *young* man outta nothin'."

It was awhile since Billy had heard worry in a woman's voice. "How much do I owe you for the meal?" he asked.

Lottie gave his arm a friendly pat. "That'll be twenty cents, American money."

"How 'bout if I decided to take along a slice of that pie after all?" Billy did have a sweet tooth.

She smiled. "Then I'd ask you for another nickel, which'd total it up to a quarter."

"Well, in that case, let's add pie to the tab." He dropped a half dollar onto the table.

"I *figured* a fella who looked like he jus' might still be a-growing'd find it hard to pass up a piece of Lottie Charbunneau's mincemeat pie."

Billy ate his pie as he rode over to First Street, past the Probity Depot, and north for another quarter of a mile.

The mechanic's shack was a huge frame building with massive double doors. There was a set of tracks that came off the main line that ran through town, and this side track went through the building length-wise, connecting again to the main line on the far end. Leading away from the side track was another, shorter line of track that ran back along the rear of the yards to the east.

Billy approached the mechanic's shack and pulled up in front of a door marked "Office." Once he was there, he dismounted, tied off Badger, and walked in.

Inside the office was a group of four men sitting at a table playing Texas Forty-two. It didn't surprise Billy to see railroaders loafing that way in the middle of the day. It had been his experience if a train crew was between shifts or for whatever reason not actually out riding the rails, they were generally hunched over a set of dominoes.

As Billy came in, they squinted up at him through their tobacco smoke, but none of them offered him anything more than a casual glance.

"Hello, fellas," Billy said. "Would one of you gents happen to be Mr. Gruber?"

A medium-sized man with eyebrows that set above his features like a couple of bushy awnings slapped a double-six down next to three other black-and-white tiles in the center of the table. "There she is, boys," he said, "bad news for you." He shouted this with a broad grin. "And that makes it eight-four."

The man sitting across from this fella let out a loud, "Hoorah," and the other two men at the table both spat strings of profanity that seemed colorful even by railroader standards.

"Who is it you said you was looking for, son?" the man with the bushy eyebrows asked. His long teeth were clasped around the soggy end of a cigar.

"Mr. Gruber, Fritz Gruber."

The man had already turned his attention back to the game. "Shuffle them bastards up good now, Tommy, Goddamn it." Then to Billy, he said, "Gruber? Hell, that big Heinie's around here somewhere, but who knows where." He offered no more information than that.

Billy, not bothering to thank the man, turned and went back out, letting the screen door slam behind him. Hooking his thumbs in his belt, he scrutinized the area. This must have been the slow time of day at the Probity train yards. There was no activity anywhere that Billy could see.

Figuring there was nothing going on here, he decided to ride to the other end of the long building and have a look. He untied Badger, and just as he started to mount up, he heard someone whistling a kind of tuneless ditty. He gave the horse's neck a couple of soothing strokes, flipped the reins back over the hitching rail, and followed the sound around the corner of the building where he spotted a burly man carrying an oil can with a long, thin spout. As the man whistled, he squirted oil from the can over a large bed of thistles growing along the track that ran behind the building. This track held a line of half a dozen two-man hand carts.

It seemed to Billy using oil was a pretty expensive way to kill thistles, but he guessed it didn't matter much to this fella since it was doubtful he was the one who paid for the oil.

"Excuse me, mister. Can you tell me where I can find Fritz Gruber?"

The thistle-killer answered by giving his head a jerk to the left in the direction of a man working on a hand cart at the other end of the line.

"Thanks," said Billy.

As Billy walked down the short length of track, all he could see of the man were his two legs sticking out from beneath the wheels of the cart. And, Billy thought, judging by the length of those legs, this fella was one long drink of water.

A German shepherd puppy, maybe eight or ten weeks old, crawled around on the man's enormous feet, gnawing his sharp puppy teeth into the man's shoes but unable to make the slightest mark on the shoes' thick leather soles.

Billy bent over in an effort to peer under the cart. "Excuse me, sir, might you be Mr. Gruber?"

"Vot?" Clearly startled, the man's big feet jerked, and the puppy went sailing. Undeterred, the little dog yipped a couple of times and attacked again.

"Sorry to disturb you, sir, but are you Mr. Fritz Gruber?"

"*Ja*," answered the accented voice. "Hi-yam Grubah. Who iss day-yah?"

"My name's Billy Young, Mr. Gruber, and I'd like to visit with you for a bit, if I could."

Slowly, this giant squeezed himself out from beneath the cart and uncoiled his way up to his full height. Billy had to lift his head so high to look into the man's broad face that he could feel the back of his hat brim nudge itself against his spine.

Fritz Gruber was enormous—at least six foot eight with shoulders as wide as an ax handle was long.

"I voot shake you han', but . . ." He smiled, shrugged, and held up ham-sized paws that were caked black with grease. He reached in the back pocket of his overalls and pulled out a rag that had once been red but was now almost as black as his hands. He made an attempt at wiping the grease away, but it was hopeless.

"I hate to bother you, Mr. Gruber, but I was wondering if I could maybe visit with you for a couple of minutes."

"Shoo-wah."

Now the puppy was hopping around Billy's feet, nipping at his pants legs.

"*Begleiter*," Gruber called out, "*nein*." He reached down and picked up the pup, which wriggled and squirmed at first but settled into Gruber's arm after a bit and began to lick his face. "Ah, Beggy," the big man cooed. "You issa goot *hund*." He closed his eyes and allowed the puppy to lap away.

"What I'd like to visit with you about is a fella by the name of Jeets Duvall."

Fritz Gruber's eyes popped open. "Jeets Duvall?"

"That's right, sir. I was told Duvall and another fella named Baxter used to work for you here at the train yards."

Gruber's eyes narrowed. "If you iss friend off Duvall—"

"No, no, I'm not his friend, but I do want to find him, sir, for my own purposes."

"Jeets Duvall iss *verrückt*. He iss crazy."

"That sure may be," said Billy, "but being crazy won't save him."

"Safe him?"

Billy hesitated about saying more, but went on anyway. "I'll be extracting a price from Jeets Duvall for the murder of my brother." He paused, then added, "And others."

Without expression, Fritz Gruber looked down at Billy. After a bit, he nodded. "You iss right. Duvall vuhked he-yah *und* Baxtah, too, but dey shhdeal dools."

Billy wasn't sure he understood. "I'm sorry, sir. They what?"

"Dey shhdeal *der* dools vom shop—renges *und* hommers *und* der scavew drifers—*und* dey sell dem in town. Vee cannot proof dey shhdeal—" He tapped his left temple with a thick index finger. "—but Gruber know. *Ja*, I fie-yah *und* say neffah you come bag no mow-wah. I haf no shhdealers vuhk he-yah."

"How long ago was that?" Billy wondered.

"Do, tree munz. Jeets Duvall, he iss crazy-mad ven I fie-yah. He shcreams. He iss bad mun, Jeets Duvall. He kills my Greta."

"Your Greta?" Billy could see a sadness fold into the huge man's eyes.

"Greta vas *mein hund*—my dog. I haf Greta fife ye-ah. Jeets Duvall, he poisons Greta afdah I fie-yah. He trows my Greta poison meat. She hass grade pains in her." He rubbed his stomach. "Inside her guds. She die hard, my Greta, because off Jeets Duvall."

Billy had to ask. "Did you go after him when he did such a thing?"

The big man seemed ashamed and lowered his head. *"Nein,"* he said after a bit, and when he spoke, his voice was barely more than a whisper. "He iss doo crazy. *Der* mun, he iss doo crazy for Gruber."

And when he said it, Billy realized this giant was afraid of Jeets Duvall. He was more than a foot and a half taller than Jeets, and he must have outweighed him by a hundred and fifty, maybe even two hundred pounds, but that didn't matter. Billy stared at Gruber for a long moment, and as he watched him, Billy sensed this hulk was the sort who would gladly take on any dozen men if it ever came to that. Fritz Gruber was no coward, but even so, he was afraid of Jeets Duvall.

For the first time, Billy felt a twinge of apprehension. But that twinge only lasted for a moment. He stopped it in its tracks. He refused to let it in.

"Do you have any idea where I can find Duvall?" Billy asked.

The big man's eyes came away from his dog and locked on Billy. "You go afdah him?"

Billy nodded.

Gruber seemed to think about that for a moment before he answered, "Hi-yam hearing he *und* hiss friend, Baxtah, dey vas cowboys out at Lovett place. Dat's big spread upriver 'bout tree miles. Lovett hass god land on bode sides off *der* river, but house *und* buildin's iss on *der* soud bank."

"Thank you, sir," Billy said, touching his hat brim. "I'll let you return to your work now, but I sure do appreciate all your help."

Billy turned and headed back toward his horse, and as he got to the corner of the building, he glanced back over his shoulder. The big man still stood there cradling his puppy as he watched Billy leave.

Chapter Six

Billy kept Badger at a trot as he followed the North Platte upstream. He was eager to locate Jeets Duvall, but Badger had already covered a lot of ground that day, and Billy held to an easy pace.

Besides, it was a pleasant ride. Billy had grown up on this river, but he had never spent any time around this particular stretch, and it was nice. Flowing through this part of Wyoming, the North Platte was the wettest spot in an otherwise arid, desolate land. Of course, those folks who came first staked their claims here along the river. The later settlers were forced to make do with harsher, drier places.

Just as Fritz Gruber had said, after about three miles he came to the Lovett place. There was a tall gate made of pine logs, and atop the gate, formed in steel, was what Billy assumed to be both the name of the ranch as well as the ranch's brand: the Rocking L.

Billy rode through the gate, and a couple of hundred yards up ahead, nestled along the river, was the operation's headquarters. There were a series of well-tended outbuildings—barns, bunkhouses, sheds, corrals. And built among the cottonwoods was a large, handsome house.

A couple of men were in one of the corrals doctoring a horse. Even from a distance, Billy could see they were not the two men he sought, but if Jeets Duvall was a hand on this place, as

Gruber had said, these fellas would know where Billy could find him.

The two men were working on a white-stockinged sorrel that had a stitched-up cut on its right foreleg. They were applying some sort of greasy balm to the cut, and as Billy rode up, they both looked his way.

"Afternoon, boys," Billy said. His experience on the train had made him cautious. Not wanting to be shot by Duvall from some hiding place, he scanned the yard and other buildings. There didn't seem to be anyone else around.

One man was holding the hoof as the other painted the horse's injury. It was the man holding the hoof who returned Billy's greeting. "Afternoon, mister," he said.

They both appeared to be a few years older than Billy and were clearly working cowboys. They wore heavy chaps. Their hats were tall with wide brims. Long droopy mustaches framed their mouths, and around their ears, their hair was cut close to their skulls. The one who had spoken was thin-boned but wiry. His thick muscles looked as though they might have been applied by a mason with a trowel. He had a fair complexion and his mustache was blond. His partner's mustache was black.

Except for the chaps and mustaches, Billy recognized that both of these fellas looked a whole lot like him. Billy was working on a mustache himself. He had been for a while, but his was yet to grow long and droopy.

"What brings you to the Rocking L, mister?" the blond mustachioed man asked. "Do you have some business with Mr. Lovett?"

"Not with Mr. Lovett, but I do with one of his hands."

"One of his hands, eh? Who's that?"

The blond cowboy was still the one doing the talking, but as Billy answered, he kept a wary eye on both of the men. These fellas worked with Duvall. It was possible they were his friends.

61

"Jeets Duvall," Billy said and waited for their reaction.

Their reaction came fast. They exchanged a quick look and a big laugh. "Jeets Duvall?" said blondie. "Well, you must not be an honest man, mister, if you have business with Jeets Duvall."

Billy didn't respond, and the silence that followed was awkward.

Finally the fella with the dark mustache asked, "What kind-a business do you have with that worthless son of a bitch?"

"It's of a personal nature," Billy answered. Hearing one of these two cursing Jeets made Billy sit a little easier in his saddle. "Can you tell me where I can locate him?"

"He don't work here no more. He quit yesterday morning."

"That's right," the blond man confirmed. "He told us he'd come into a considerable sum of money and his cow-punching days was through. He said he was off to do what he'd always said he was gonna do if he ever got a few dollars ahead."

"What might that be?" Billy asked.

"Buy hisself that white trash Leo Springer's large-breasted daughter and take her up to an old abandoned cabin he knows about on the La Prele." It was the fella with the black mustache who told Billy that.

They shared another hearty laugh with that one, and the blond added, "Jeets said ol' Leo wanted three hundred dollars for that girl, but Jeets figured since she was a little bit bucktoothed he could maybe get the man down to two-fifty."

Billy scrutinized these two for a moment, trying to decide if they were telling the truth. After a bit he judged they were, even though their story was one hard to believe.

Without saying more, he turned Badger toward the gate and spurred him forward.

"Hey, where ya goin', mister?" the black-mustached man called out.

"Up the La Prele."

The blond man hollered, "If yer a-plannin' on interferin' in that crazy bastard's fun, he's apt to pickle your gizzard." That remark brought on another peal of laughter.

Billy was glad he'd had a good meal at Lottie's that afternoon because he had to make a cold camp that night. He couldn't risk a fire, so all he ate was the biscuits and elk jerky he'd brought from home.

It was an hour after dark when he first located Jeets Duvall's cabin. He then backtracked a couple of hundred yards and spread his bed roll in a stand of cottonwoods next to La Prele Creek. He could see the cabin through the trees.

He wasn't sure what to do. He considered waiting until sunrise and calling the man out. That was how they dealt with killers in the dime novels he'd read. As far as Billy knew, those novels only exaggerated things a little. There were times a few years back when it was not uncommon for men to settle their grievances in that fashion. He'd heard stories about it from a few of the men who'd been around in those days, Hugo Dorling included. Even in these more civilized times, it happened some. Billy knew men who still prided themselves in the speed and accuracy with which they could pull their weapons and fire. He and Frank used to practice that themselves out behind the barn, and they got pretty fair at it, too.

But Billy never seriously considered the idea of calling Jeets Duvall out for an old-fashioned gunfight. Even if he did, he knew as soon as he made his presence known, Jeets would shoot him from a window. The man might be stupid and crazy, but Billy doubted he was a fool, at least not that much of a fool.

Jeets's having a girl with him also complicated things. If it weren't for the girl, Billy could sneak down there, kick in the door, and kill the man straight out. But if he did that with the girl in the small cabin, when Billy kicked in the door, he would have to make sure the person he was firing at was Jeets Duvall and not her, an action that might cost him enough precious time that it would turn out to be Billy who ended up getting shot rather than Jeets.

No, Billy decided, there was only one way to settle things with Duvall. Take his rifle, move through the trees a little closer to the cabin, and in the morning when Jeets came outside to relieve himself, put a bullet into him. A simple plan.

That was the smart way, but Billy's first reaction to that idea was distaste. It was not the thought of killing a man that troubled him. He had killed the onion-eater, Noah Baxter, and felt fine about it. To his surprise, he had even taken pleasure in doing it. No, Billy was sure he could gladly kill Baxter, Jeets, and their leader, too; that was not the problem. It was sniping a man while hiding behind cover that bothered him. It seemed to be the coward's way.

He pulled a piece of jerky from his saddle bag and stepped to the creek to dip his cup in the water. He leaned against a tree and bit off a piece of the dried, seasoned meat. It was tasty. Orozco made the best elk jerky in the county. Billy had killed this elk last fall on a hunting trip he and Frank had taken up the mountain.

He washed the meat down with a sip of the cool creek water. He still couldn't think about Frank. Not now. Not tonight. Soon he was going to kill one of Frank's murderers. And even if the manner in which the chore was to be performed was distasteful, Billy would do it the smart way—the same way he would kill an animal.

About nine o'clock, Billy climbed into his bedroll and tried to sleep. It'd been a long day with a lot of riding, but his thoughts were racing, and he couldn't seem to shut them down.

After an hour or so of tossing and turning, he climbed from

under his blankets and pulled his Marlin Eighty-one from its scabbard.

The waxing gibbous moon provided Billy with plenty of light to make his way along the creek and through the trees toward the dilapidated cabin. The cottonwoods grew within fifty yards of the rough front door, and Billy settled himself behind a boulder and waited.

The cabin was a sorry place. It was made of pine logs and once might have been a suitable shelter, but those days were long ago. It looked to have been abandoned for years. Much of the chinking had fallen away, and the corner of the roof on the far side had started to fold inward.

Billy could see the dull yellow blot of a coal-oil lamp through the thin, weathered material of a gunny-sack curtain. And faintly, just beneath the chirp of the crickets, he could hear the murmur of voices.

What kind of a man, Billy wondered, would sell his daughter? And what must the girl have been going through since Jeets Duvall brought her to this cabin? That thought almost brought Billy to his feet, but he forced himself to stay put. Rushing the place and getting both himself and the girl killed was not the way to go.

He would hold off and do the job as planned.

As he waited for morning, Billy slipped in and out of a light sleep. It was during one of these dozings that he heard the snap of a branch behind him. In one fluid move, he swung around and positioned himself on his right knee with the rifle at his shoulder aimed in the direction of the sound.

"Hold it, mister, don't shoot," someone whispered from the brush. "It's a friend, not a foe."

"Come out into the moonlight," Billy whispered back, "and keep your hands where I can see 'em."

The bush moved, and the black mustached cowboy stepped

into sight. It was the man from earlier that day who had cursed Jeets Duvall. He looked as he had that afternoon, except his work gloves were off and tucked into his gun belt.

"I ain't sure what it is you're planning, mister," the cowboy said, "but I had the feeling when we met at the ranch today that you hunting Jeets the way you are is on account of some grudge."

"So," Billy said, "what's it to you?"

"It ain't nothing to me, really, 'cept ever since Jeets come in yesterday and quit, I've been thinking about him and that girl. I know Jeets Duvall, mister, and I can't keep from thinking about Leo Springer's daughter." He looked down at the dirt. "I guess I could've come up here on my own. I was wrestlin' with it, but the truth is I was afraid to try anything by myself. I decided with the two of us, though, maybe we could make something of it. I spotted your horse and camp downstream a ways. I tied my pony with yours and came on up. I'd like to give you a hand, if you're willing."

Billy gave the idea a quick rundown, and after a bit, he lifted the Marlin's muzzle and eased the hammer down. "All right," he said, "I reckon I could use the help."

When the muzzle went up, the cowboy's hands came down, and a wide grin spread beneath his wider mustaches. "Whew," he said, giving his head a little shake, "I don't mind telling you, mister, it brings on a discomforting feeling when you're staring into the barrel of a rifle." He bent low and joined Billy behind the boulder. "Name's Chester Black, at your service." He stuck out his hand and Billy shook it.

"I'm Billy Young from over by Casper Mountain. Before you get into this too deep, Mr. Black, you should know what I intend to do. Two days ago Jeets and a couple of other fellas robbed a train and murdered seven people. One of the ones they murdered was my elder brother."

"I figured it might be something like that. I'm sorry to hear it. I reckon that explains how Jeets came by his sudden riches."

"You should also realize, Mr. Black, while you can still change your mind, that I do not intend to capture Jeets Duvall. I don't intend to take him to the law for trial. What I do intend is to show him no mercy."

"I understand."

"I intend to kill him, and if you would rather not be a party to such a thing, it'd be better if you returned to your horse."

"You do whatever you have to do, Mr. Young. I'm here for the girl."

Billy nodded. "All right, sir, as long as we're clear."

"We are, and I accept whatever it is you plan."

Billy leaned against the boulder and pulled a strip of the jerky from his pocket, broke it in two, and handed one of the pieces to Black. "Here you go," he said. "We might as well make ourselves comfortable. What I aim to do is wait until Jeets comes out in the morning and plug 'im from here."

"Hell," Black said as he bit into the meat, "it don't sound like you're gonna need my help at all."

"Well," said Billy, "you never know. Sometimes plans go sour."

"Yep," agreed the cowboy, "ain't it the truth."

"I'm not proud of doing it this way, but Jeets is a dangerous man."

"He is at that."

"How well do you know him?" Billy asked.

"Not well, really. He's worked at the Rocking L for a couple of months. Showed up one day in the late spring with his riding partner, Noah Baxter, and we put 'em both to work. Which reminds me, was Baxter involved with the robbery?"

"He was," Billy said. "Him, I was able to kill."

"Well, I'll be. I wondered where he was yesterday when Jeets came 'round. You never see one without t'other."

"They were with a third man when they robbed the train.

Did you ever see them running with another fella?"

"Nah, can't say as I have."

"He was a man a little bigger than me. He wore a fancy vest and his gun low."

"Well, wait, you know, I did see the two of them talking to a fella matching that description one day last week. We was moving some cows out of the hills back down to the home place, and this fella rode out and met us. He pulled Jeets and Baxter aside, and they all had a chat. He wasn't there more than five, ten minutes at the most, and then he rode off."

"Any idea who he was?"

"Nah, never saw him before or since. I asked Baxter about it later, and he said it was just a fella wanting them to do a little work on the side."

"A little work like train robbery. I wonder why he would even think about hooking up with those two in the first place?"

Black shook his head. "You got me, friend. A couple of days later, all of us boys was in the cook shack eatin' our supper, and Jeets told Baxter to hurry up, they had to go meet Zeke Blood. Now, I don't know if this Blood was the same fella they was talking to before, but I reckon it could've been."

"Blood," repeated Billy, "strange name."

"It ain't common, I reckon. But it ain't unheard of. I knew a family of Bloods down on the Sweetwater when I was a kid. This fella weren't from Wyoming, though. Baxter mentioned something about him being from Texas."

Zeke Blood. Something told Billy, after Jeets, this was the next man he needed to find.

As that thought spun around, a sound came from the direction of the cabin, and Billy turned away from the cowboy to take a look.

"Can you see anything?" Black whispered.

"Someone's coming out." The sun was still below the horizon, but the eastern sky was lit, and when the man stepped through the door, Billy could see that it was, in fact, the train robber and killer, Jeets Duvall. "It's him," Billy said, "sure enough."

The time had finally come. Billy lifted the Marlin and settled the stock into his shoulder. The little man made a small but easy target. Billy took in a breath and pulled back the rifle's hammer. He laid the front sight over Jeets's dark heart, and just as he brought the rear sight in line with the front, he heard the triple click of another hammer being cocked. A second later he felt a muzzle nudge his ear.

"Put that rifle down, Mr. Young. And put 'er down extra slow."

CHAPTER SEVEN

"Hey, Jeets," Black called out. "It's Chester Black from the Rocking L."

Jeets had already begun to take care of his morning business, but when Black shouted his name, Jeets was able to shut down his water, spin around on the balls of his bare feet, and sprint for the cabin, tucking his parts back into his pants as he ran.

"It's all right, Jeets," Black called out again. "You're safe. There was a fella here who meant you harm, but I got him held at gunpoint."

By this time, Jeets was inside, and the stubby double-barrels of a sawed-off shotgun emerged from the window to the left of the cabin's door.

"Come out to the clearin' and show yourselves," Jeets shouted.

"Do as he says, Mr. Young."

Billy stood, and as he came up, Black lifted Billy's short-barreled Colt out of its holster and tucked it into the top of his chaps. Bending down, he picked up the rifle.

Billy stepped from the cover of the rock, his hands in the air, and Chester Black came behind.

"Everything's fine now, Jeets. Everything's under control."

"Who is that fella, anyhow?" Jeets asked.

"Let us come in and I'll tell you all about it."

"Come ahead, but do 'er easy. I'm-a watchin' yer ev'ry step."

"Go on," Black said, giving Billy a shove.

"You're a lying scum, Black."

"Not really. I told you the truth. I came here for the girl. That's all I want." As they neared the door, he gave Billy another shove, causing him to trip and fall into the dank, rancid-smelling cabin.

"What's this all about?" Jeets asked once they were inside. He still held the shotgun, but he held it low in the crook of his arm. "Who is this fella?" He squinted at Billy for a better look. "You seem familiar, mister. What's yer name?"

"His name's Billy Young, Jeets."

"That don't mean squat to me."

"He says you and Baxter, along with another fella, killed his brother."

"Hell," Jeets said with a smile, "I've killed a lotta folks' brothers."

"I guess you boys musta killed his brother just a couple of days ago when you was robbin' a train."

Jeets stiffened and aimed at Chester Black the dark gaze he'd been holding on Billy. "What do you know about a train robbery?"

"Just what this fella here told me," Black said. "Nothin' more and I don't wanna know nothin' more. All I know is not three minutes ago this fella here was pointing this here Marlin at you while you were standing outside with nothin' in your hand but your whacker." He set the rifle against the wall. "If it weren't for me, you would be a dead man."

Jeets turned again to Billy. "Is that true, boy? Were you about to kill ol' Jeets?"

"I was," Billy said, "and I'll do it yet."

Jeets and Black both got a good laugh out of Billy's bodacious threat.

"I doubt it," Jeets said and raised the shotgun. "I recognize you now. It were you and that other fella that knocked me off my horse. You're the pup who put a thirty-thirty slug into Noah, my good friend and partner. I don't know whether to kill you outright or a piece at a time."

Black, who by now had edged his way to the side and a step behind Jeets, said, "Hold on, now, Jeets, he ain't yours to kill, not yet, anyhow. He's mine. I captured him. He belongs to me."

"The hell you say."

Billy could see the muscles of Jeets' forearm begin to flex as the little man tightened his finger on the trigger.

"I mean it, Jeets," Black said, and he leveled his pistol at Jeets's temple.

"You gonna shoot me, Chester?" Jeets asked.

Billy could tell Black was nervous, but despite having a forty-five nestled against the side of his head, Jeets Duvall seemed to be having fun.

"I hope it don't come to that, Jeets, but I'll do 'er if I must. I'm here to offer you a trade."

"A trade? What kinda trade?"

"I'll let you kill this fella here if you let me have some of that girl you bought yesterday. I have wanted some of her ever since the first time I laid eyes on her."

Jeets seemed confused. "You wanna take my little Jill?" he asked.

"I don't mean to take her for keeps. I just want to borrow her for maybe a day or two, and I'll give her back."

"Give 'er back the worse for wear, I'd wager."

"I wouldn't hurt her much," Black said. "Where is she, anyhow?"

"She's right over yonder in the corner. Take a look for yer-self."

Both Black and Billy peered into the gloom, but Billy couldn't make out anything.

Apparently Black couldn't either. "Where?" he asked. "I don't see nothin' "

"Take the lamp and carry it over. She's just right yonder."

"First, you put the shotgun against the wall next to the Marlin and stand away."

"Sure thing, Chester. That's fine by me." Jeets propped the gun against the cabin wall and stepped back.

Black lifted the coal-oil lamp from a table, crossed the room, and shone the light into the corner.

"Well, well," Black said, "what do we have here?"

Jill Springer stood mostly naked on her tiptoes atop a small footstool. Her hands were tied behind her, exposing her full breasts. There was a rope around her neck, the end of which was tied to a ring that had been hammered into the wall near the ceiling. The rope was about six feet long, but it was tied off short, pulling the girl's neck and back up flush against the wall.

It was clear to Billy why she hadn't made any sounds. The rope was tight enough around her neck she could barely breathe. Speaking would be impossible. Her face was a mass of cuts and bruises. Her left eye was swollen shut. Dark marks ran up and down her body. It appeared Jeets had paid particular attention to her breasts.

"Hell, Jeets," Black said in what came out in something close to a whine, "you only had her a little more than a day, and it looks to me like you damned near ruined her."

"Oh, no, I did not." Jeets sounded offended. "Take a good look at her. She's got plenty left."

Black turned her face toward the light of the lamp. The girl's one working eye looked at him, and Billy could see by the hate that filled it that in a way Jeets was right. There was plenty of Jill Springer left.

Black let go of her face and turned to Jeets. "So, do we have a deal?"

"I might be willin' to do a little horse tradin'," Jeets said.

"Tell me again what your terms are."

"I take her to my camp and keep her for two days. I'll bring her back up here forty-eight hours from now. In exchange, you get Billy Young here to do with as you please."

Jeets seemed to ponder the offer. "Two days is a long time," he finally said. "I'll give you one. Fact is, I won't even give you one." He pulled a watch from his pocket, and Billy recognized it as the watch the fancy-dressed man had dropped into the mailbag on the day of the robbery. "It's goin' on five o'clock right now." He snapped the watch closed and dropped it back into his pocket. "I'll give 'er to you for twelve hours. You have 'er back by five o'clock this afternoon."

"Twelve hours? That ain't enough."

Jeets laughed. "The hell it ain't. Why, that girl will wear you out in half that time."

Black still held his pistol, and Jeets' shotgun was better than six feet away. "What's to keep me from just shootin' you down and takin' her for my own?"

Jeets laughed again. " 'Cause you ain't got the gumption. That's why. If you had the spunk, you'd-a done it when you had your forty-five poked up against the side of my noggin, and we'd-a never been havin' this conversation in the first place." He winked. "That's what I'd-a done. You betcha. That's what Jeets Duvall would-a done, but you ain't got the stuff, Mr. Black." He reached down and squeezed his crotch obscenely. "You ain't got enough-a this."

Billy could tell by Black's expression that he wanted to lift his forty-five and shoot the smile off Jeets Duvall's face, but the cowboy couldn't dig up what it takes. Jeets might've been dumb, but he knew what a man needed for murder and who was capable and who was not.

"Now you count your stars that I'm-a feelin' generous enough to give you the loan of my sweetheart for as long as I am." He

74

looked over and offered the girl a feral grin. "I wouldn't be willin' to do it, 'cept she's got me plum tuckered out and I need my rest. She'll have you that way too long before your twelve hours is up."

There was a silence, and Billy could see the conversation was over.

"All right, Jeets. You gotta deal. Twelve hours it'll be." He dropped his gun into his holster, reached over, untied the girl from the wall, and pulled her off the stool. "Where's her shoes?" Black asked. "She can't walk down to the camp barefoot."

"Damned if I know," said Jeets, "but they gotta be 'round here somewheres. She was shod when I brought her in. Look over there against the far wall. That's where I tossed her stuff."

Black started for the spot where Jeets was pointing but stopped himself short. "Hold on a second. I ain't turning my back on you nor him neither one." He nodded toward Billy, who during the argument over the girl had inched his way closer to the shotgun and rifle leaning against the wall. "And Young, get your ass back over there across the room away from them weapons." He brought his hand to the butt of his holstered forty-five, and Billy did as he was told. "You, Jeets, go over and fetch her shoes yourself. I'm stayin' right here."

Jeets threw his hands in the air and let them slap against the outsides of his thighs in a kind of good-natured frustration. "For Christ's sake, Chester, I said we had us a deal. I'm lettin' ya take my little dumplin' right outta the cabin here to use in whatever vile manner you choose. What more can a man do?"

Black smiled. "You can fetch-up them shoes, and we'll be on our way."

Jeets shook his head. "All right, all right. Here, give me the damned light." He took the lantern and crossed to the far wall where he began to rummage through a pile of clothes—coats, hats, pants, and dresses—some apparently belonged to Jeets', some belonged to the girl. "I couldn't get that cheap bastard Springer to come off his three-hundred-dollar price tag for little Jill there, but at least I did get him to throw in a couple of old, ragged dresses and even a slab of bacon." He continued to dig through the pile, cursing as he did. "Well," he said after a bit, "here the damned things are."

He stood and turned, holding a long, blue, eighteen-fifty-one Navy Colt revolver. Before Black could speak or move or even let out a cuss, Jeets cocked and fired. The ball from the old gun struck the cowboy square in the center of his chest, knocking him flat on his back.

When Black hit the floor, Billy moved for the sawed-off against the wall.

"Hold it," Jeets shouted, turning the Navy on him. Billy stopped in his tracks. "That's a good boy. Now you stand right there and behave yersef."

Jeets went over to the prone but still breathing Chester Black. With Black's every breath, the hole in his chest spewed blood like a tiny red geyser. Black's eyes were clenched, and he was calling on both Jesus and his mother.

"Hush that damned jabberin'," Jeets said.

Black went silent and his eyes popped open. Despite his wound, his features were alert.

"Did you really think ol' Jeets was gonna let you take away his sweetie pie? I ain't that kinda man, Mr. Black. Why, I just weren't raised that way." He pulled back the Navy's hammer. "Leo Springer drove a hard bargain, but, like I said before, after considerable talk I got him to toss in some of the girl's clothes, a slab of bacon, and also this here ol' Navy Colt to boot the deal." He scrutinized the large gun. "It's an antique-y ol' thing, I know, but it still works pretty good, doncha think?" And with that, he sent a ball into the front of the cowboy's skull.

Billy's ears still rang from the sound of the first shot. The roar of the second nearly burst his ears.

A blanket of blue gun smoke swirled in the air around Jeets's face. The little man fanned it away as he stared down at Chester Black. "Well," he observed, "I expect the fella is dead. I never yet met a man that could survive a lead ball passin' through the middle of his brains."

He looked toward Billy. "It is now time to reckon with you, young fella. I just remembered that not only did you kill my good *amigo*, Noah, but you also hid like a snivelin' coward behind my horse during the fracas at the train causing him to be killed as well. He was a good ol' horse. I'd had that animal for close to two years, and he never once let me down."

Billy knew his situation was hopeless, but that did not slacken his rage—the rage that had begun two days before. "Stop your gab, you repulsive dwarf, and pull the trigger. Being dead'd be better than having to listen to you." He balled his fists and took a step forward. When Billy came at him, Jeets's eyes bulged, and despite holding the gun, he took a quick step backward.

But Jeets's surprise at Billy's aggression lasted only a second. "All right, boy," he said, peeling back a greasy smile. "I'd be happy to oblige your request. I like to shoot big 'uns like you, 'cause y'all make such a nice sound when you hit the ground."

His small thumb crooked up to the big Navy's hammer, but as it did, something hit Jeets from behind.

Billy had watched as Jill Springer lowered her shoulder and made a running dive at the small of Jeets Duvall's back, hitting him with enough force to send him lunging into Billy's waiting arms.

Billy wrapped his left hand around Jeets's right wrist and snapped it like a twig. Jeets screamed, and the Navy hit the dirt floor. Billy curled his right hand around Jeets's throat and lifted him up to eye level. He started to say something into the little man's gnarled face, but the words could not wend their way through the thicket of his rage. Instead, Billy flung the killer into the log wall on the far side of the room. When he hit, the air blew out of him with a whoosh.

Jeets raised himself to all fours, but before he could stand, Billy was across the room. He drew back his foot, kicked, and Jeets Duvall was airborne—again smashing into the wall. Once more Jeets tried to rise, and again Billy let loose with his boot, this time kicking Jeets full in the face, caving in his mouth and crushing his nose.

Jeets gagged and spit out blood and teeth. "All right," he said in a hoarse croak, "I've had enough. You got me caught."

Billy paid no attention and kicked him again, hearing Jeets's rib cage crack.

"Listen here, you son of a bitch," Jeets screamed, "you done got me. I can't take no more." Still Billy ignored the man's pleas, lifted him by his shirt, and drove his fist into the soggy mush of his face. This time when the killer hit the wall he banged the back of his head against the logs. He didn't lose consciousness, but his sand was gone, and he slithered to the dirt floor.

Billy turned, crossed the room, and came back with Jeets's own sawed-off shotgun. He pulled back both hammers. Jeets looked up with wide eyes, saw what was about to happen, and rolled himself into a ball, pleading in barely audible whispers, "Don't shoot. Don't shoot. Don't shoot."

Billy stared down at the groveling man. With one tug of both triggers, Billy could send Jeets Duvall to his maker in pieces. But he stopped himself before he pulled the triggers.

"What's wrong?" Jill Springer asked. "Aren't you gonna kill him?" She stood in the middle of the room, her small arms still behind her back the way the man on the floor had lashed them. Her head was canted to one side so she could look at Billy with her only useable eye.

Billy listened to the little man's whimpers, and then lowered the shotgun's hammers. "He's gonna hang," Billy said, and a look of relief and even victory spread across Jeets Duvall's busted features.

As Jeets watched Billy set the sawed-off aside, he seemed to regain his boldness. "I figured you didn't have the guts to do it yerself, you Nancy-boy prick."

"Are you gonna take him into Probity?" the girl asked. "Are you gonna let them hang him there?"

Billy didn't answer. Instead, he bent and picked the little man up, and when he did, Jeets screamed with the pain of his broken wrist and ribs and face. Billy dragged the murderer to the footstool where Chester Black had found the girl and stood him atop it.

"What the hell're you doin'?" Jeets's grit from a moment before had dissolved. "What the hell're you doin', Goddamn it?"

Billy's only answer was to make some slack in the rope that still dangled from the steel ring and wrap it around the man's scrawny neck.

"Jeets Duvall," Billy said, "you're not the sort who deserves to live with normal folks, and it's long past your time."

Jeets began to squirm, and Billy pulled the rope taut, drawing him up to the tip of his toes. "No, you can't do this," Jeets was able to get out through his gasps. His bloody mouth sprayed red. "By God, it ain't *legal*."

Billy nodded. "I expect you're right," he allowed.

He then kicked the stool from beneath the killer's feet.

Chapter Eight

Riding up the middle of Main Street in Probity, Wyoming, with a beat-to-hell girl on one horse and two dead men lashed to another caused a number of the small town's citizens to stop and stare.

Billy reined in and looked down at a couple of teenagers who stood in front of McConners' General Store. "Can either of you young gents tell me where I might find the sheriff?"

The smaller of the two said, "Sure, mister. Sheriff Linford's office is just around the corner. Head on down to the next street and make a left. It's in the middle of the block."

Billy touched a finger to the brim of his hat. "Thanks," he said.

As he turned the gray's head, the boy jerked his chin toward the horse carrying the bodies and asked, "Did you kill them two fellas, mister?"

"Hush up, Micah," said the bigger boy. "It's none of your business."

"Only one of 'em, kid."

"Did he deserve it?" the boy asked.

Billy nodded. "He did."

"Good for you, mister," the boy said with a smile. "Good for you."

Billy nudged the gray's flank. "Uh-huh," he said but did not return the kid's smile.

Billy had thought the death of Jeets Duvall would fill the hole that had been left when Frank was murdered, but it didn't happen. That spot was as vacant now as it had been before.

He wondered whether killing the last man would leave it as empty. But he reminded himself, whether it would or wouldn't didn't matter. Right or wrong, legal or illegal, good or bad, empty or full, none of it mattered; that man, too, would die, just as these behind him had died, just as Frank had died, just as the others at the train had died.

This, he thought, seemed to be the season for dying along the North Platte.

He and the girl found the sheriff's office around the corner, and Billy brought the horses up to the rail. Jill Springer was riding Jeets's animal, and Billy had tied the bodies to the horse Chester Black had left at the campsite.

Billy dismounted and was about to tie off the horses when a tall, lanky fella exited the sheriff's office. He was smoking a short cheroot and wore a badge pinned to his brown corduroy vest.

"What do we have here?" He seemed to be perturbed by a man he did not know hauling a couple of corpses to his doorstep. Billy couldn't blame him.

Billy nodded toward the dead men. "The fella tied in front there's named—"

"I know who *they* are," said the sheriff, eyeing the bodies. "It's you I ain't never seen before."

"Well, sir, that's true. You haven't." He flipped Badger's reins around the rail, then did the same with the other reins he held. "The name's Billy Young. My family owns—" He stopped himself and cleared his throat. "I own a place at the foot of Casper Mountain. I was in search of the little one there. I killed him shortly after he killed the other fella. The one I was after was a train robber and a murderer and a purchaser of young girls. The second fella was a scoundrel himself only not so bad as the first."

"I know that runt Duvall," said the sheriff. "You, I don't know, but if you say Duvall robbed and killed, I'd believe it because I know his character. Chester Black I never knew to be a scoundrel, but I've been sheriffing long enough that there ain't much surprises me."

"Well, sir, I never met him myself before yesterday. I only call him a scoundrel because it was his intention to rape and abuse this girl here." He glanced toward Jill Springer.

The sheriff looked up at Jill sitting atop Jeets's horse. "Jill, is that you?"

The girl nodded and stared at the horse's mane.

"My God, girl, what happened?"

"She fell into the hands of Jeets Duvall," Billy said. "Her father sold her to him for three hundred dollars, which, I imagine, is apt to be a crime of some sort, at least since the days of Mr. Lincoln."

"I expect you're right. Come into the office, Mr. Young, and you can tell me your story. You too, Jill." He turned to a kid who was standing close by. "You, boy," he said, "fetch Mr. Somerhill. Tell him he has some business waiting for him here in front of my office." He tossed the boy a penny. "Now, don't you be going over to McConners' and buying stick candy with that money until you fetch the mortician. Do you hear me?"

"Yes, sir, Sheriff." He turned on his bare heel and scampered away.

"Come on inside. There's coffee on the stove."

Fifteen minutes later, Billy was on his second cup of coffee and had told his story starting at the train robbery and going through all the events in the cabin. Jill confirmed as true the parts she knew about. As it happened, the sheriff had already been informed of the robbery.

"I heard about it day before yesterday when Mirabel Simms got a telegram from Casper telling of the holdup and that her husband, Bernard, had been one of the victims."

When the sheriff mentioned that, Billy remembered the fancy-dressed man had boarded the train at the Probity stop.

"I know which one he was," Billy said. He reached into his pocket and pulled out a watch. "This was his watch. I took it off Jeets Duvall's body."

"The authorities in Casper are shipping Bernard home on the afternoon train." He checked his own watch. "In fact, it should be pulling into the station in less than half an hour. Mirabel will be there to meet it. Maybe you should take his watch over and give it to her. I expect it'd mean a lot."

"I'll do it, Sheriff. It might comfort her some to hear from a person who was with her husband when he died."

Sheriff Linford stood and walked to a small stove in the corner. "More coffee?"

"None for me," Billy said, "and it looks like Jill didn't even finish her first cup." After Billy had explained to the sheriff how he came to possess two dead men tied to a horse, Jill had gone to sit on a large horse-hair couch sitting against the wall. She was now asleep. "It was a hard time for her back in the cabin."

"I can see that," said the sheriff. "Do you think I should fetch the doc?"

"No, she just needs some rest, and a place to stay, too, I reckon. She can't go back to her father's."

Linford poured himself another cup and stood looking out the window. "Maybe she can't go out to her father's, but I sure can. I'll see to it Leo Springer goes to prison for what he's done."

"Prison sounds like a fine place for him," Billy agreed.

The sheriff still had his back to Billy as he watched the passing traffic. "Here comes Somerhill for the bodies now." He took a sip of his coffee. "It's been a busy week for that fella. I always heard death comes in threes. It looks to be coming in fives for Probity this week."

"Why? Who else died?" Billy asked.

"Well, there's these two and the skunk, Noah Baxter—" The sheriff returned to his desk and sat down. "—number four'd be Bernie Simms. Those're all related to the robbery, of course, either direct or indirect. Then just three days ago Caldwell Unger, one of our local lawyers, was killed."

"Oh, yes," Billy said. "I heard about that. It was a hunting accident, wasn't it?"

"Yep, that's what it looks like, I reckon."

"You don't sound too sure."

The sheriff popped a wooden match into flame with his thumbnail and applied it to the tip of his stubby cigar. The cigar was short enough Billy wondered whether the man might set his nose on fire. "There are some things about it that don't seem right," the sheriff said as he shook out the match. He held the cigar between his clenched teeth, and smoke escaped in little puffs as he spoke.

"Like what?" Billy asked. He was almost as exhausted as Jill, and it felt good to sit and relax with a warm cup of coffee and talk about something other than his own concerns.

"Well, it's all over town, so I don't guess it'd hurt anything to mention it now, but Caldwell Unger hadn't gone hunting in years. He used to say why in the world would a man want to eat a piece of stringy, wild-tasting venison—or, even worse yet, antelope—when he had unlimited access to good Wyoming beef."

"I'm a hunter," Billy allowed, "but I'm also a cattleman, so the man's logic makes sense to me, especially the part about antelope. I never could develop a taste for goat."

"That ain't all. Caldwell went off on this hunt in the middle of the day wearing a pair of dress shoes and his business suit. According to his wife, the old Spencer Repeater he took along was more a decoration than anything else. It'd been hanging on the wall in his office for years, and she knew for a fact he never even kept any ammunition for it."

"Did Mr. Unger have any enemies?"

"Hell, boy, he was a lawyer. What d'you think? But I know what you're getting at, and the thought crossed my mind, too. I figure as far as lawyers go, Caldwell Unger was pretty well liked. He was the most successful lawyer around. So, no, I don't think there's any reason to suspect foul play, but it is awful strange."

"Did his wife say why she thought he might've decided to go hunting?"

"She couldn't understand it, but I didn't get to talk to her about it too much. She left yesterday right after the funeral— went back to Nebraska to be with her sister for a while."

"Well, you're right, it is a little strange, isn't it?" Billy said.

"Yes, sir, it is at that. But Cal was an odd one, always had been. He liked doing things his own way. That's for sure." The sheriff blew a stream of smoke at the ceiling. "You know, it's hard on a town to have this many deaths so close together, even if a couple of 'em are men the likes of Jeets Duvall and Noah Baxter. It's hard on folks' spirit to be reminded of death too often."

Billy knew it was true. He'd seen enough death in the last three days to last him the rest of his life, but he knew that what he had seen was not all he would see before he was done. "Did you ever hear of a fella around these parts by the name of Blood, Zeke Blood?" he asked

"Blood, you say?"

"Yes. If he's who I think he is, he was one of the outlaws who robbed the train with Duvall and Baxter. He was the leader of the bunch, and the man who killed my brother."

The sheriff flicked an ash in the general direction of a tin ashtray on his desk. "Nope, never heard of the man. I'm pretty sure there's no one by that name from around here."

Jill rolled over on the couch, and when she did, she let out a soft moan. Perhaps it was a moan caused by the pain from her many bruises, or perhaps it was from some pain caused by a dream. "I'd like to make some arrangements for the girl," Billy said. "Got any suggestions on where she might could live?"

The sheriff took a long sip of his coffee. Billy expected this fella drank a lot more coffee in a day than he ever did water. "Well, sir, you know I might at that. It seems I heard Mrs. Jordan was looking for a girl to help out over at her boarding house. I don't know what the pay is, for sure, but I know it includes room and board. It might be just the thing."

"Yes, sir, it might. Maybe we'll give it a try, if Jill's willing."

He stood, set his empty mug on the sheriff's desk, and crossed to the couch. He bent and gave Jill's shoulder a gentle shake. She woke with a start, her eyes wide and fearful.

"It's all right, Jill," he said. "It's just me, Billy." It seemed to take a moment for what he said to register, but when it did, she gave a brief, almost embarrassed, smile and rubbed her one working eye. "We have to go now," Billy said, and she nodded and stood.

"Thanks for your help, Sheriff. And I'll take Mr. Simms's watch to his wife over at the depot. What time did you say the train'll be coming in?"

Sheriff Linford rose from his chair and walked them to the door. "S'posed to be here at one-seventeen, but it's a train, and they've been known to run late." As they stepped out onto the boardwalk, he said, "I plan to have me a visit with your pa, Jill."

The girl didn't respond.

"I promise you, he won't be botherin' you ever again."

When Billy stepped off the sidewalk, Mortician Somerhill

was untying the rope that lashed Jeets to the back of Chester Black's horse, so Billy gave the man a hand loading him into his hearse.

"Thank you, son," the dark-suited man said as he tipped his derby. "I got to hurry and get these two over to the parlor because I have another body coming in on the train in fifteen minutes." Somerhill made the statement with what appeared to Billy to be a practiced solemnity, but Billy thought he might have also heard just a hint of greed beneath the man's grave tones.

As it happened, Mrs. Jordan did have a position for a maid at her boarding house, and she hired Jill right then. The woman was a widow in her mid-thirties who, the sheriff had explained earlier, had been left a large house when her husband died of consumption three years before.

After she showed Jill to her room, the girl came downstairs and met Billy on the front porch.

"I want to thank you. I don't know what would have become of me," she said, "if it weren't for you."

Billy smiled. "Well, now, Jill, if you hadn't rammed your shoulder into the middle of Jeets Duvall's back, I expect I could say the same thing, except I *do* know what would've become of me. I'd be carrying the extra weight of one of the little killer's Navy Colt balls either between my eyes or in some other tender location."

She tried to return his smile, but it wouldn't quite form. Billy could see beneath her injuries Jill Springer was a pretty girl. She had thick chestnut hair with a natural wave to it that folded itself down the side of her face. Her eyes were the color of a mountain lake on a sunny afternoon. Her nose was thin and straight with sharp, well-defined nostrils. Her lips were soft and full. Yes, sir, take away the cuts and bruises, and Jill Springer was very pretty.

She wouldn't look him directly in the eye, and he sensed it was because of the way he had seen her—bound and mostly nude, raped, and beaten. He reached down and lifted her face with his index finger. Again, she tried to smile, and for the first time Billy noticed she had just the tiniest bit of an overbite. It was a small imperfection that provided balance to her otherwise fine features.

"You're going to be all right, Jill. You don't have to feel bad about what happened. You didn't do anything wrong. Do you believe me?"

She nodded, and a single tear leaked from her swollen left eye. "Yes," she said, but Billy doubted she meant it. He suspected it would be a while before all of Jill's wounds would heal.

"What I'm going to do, Jill, is take Jeets's and Chester Black's horses and tack over to the livery stable and tell the fella there to sell them and to give the money to you."

"You don't have to do that."

"Yes," Billy said, "I do. You deserve it. Besides, you're on your own now, and you'll need to have whatever money you can get your hands on." He reached into his pocket. "Here's another forty-three dollars. This came off Jeets. Chester Black was flat broke, or I'd give you what he had as well." He held the money out to her. She shook her head. "Yes," Billy insisted, "you take it."

She took it, but said, "I really don't think I'll need it, Billy, what with the money from the horses and my new job." She looked toward the front door of the large house. "Mrs. Jordan seems nice, doesn't she?"

"Yes, she does."

"She says I'll be mostly cleaning rooms and washing dishes, at least at first, but later on she wants me to do some cooking, too. I'm a good cook, you know. I used to cook for Pa—" Her voice choked off, and she fell against Billy's chest, her body shuddering with sobs. "I'm a good girl," she whispered.

Billy held her close.

Chapter Nine

Billy hoped the train from Casper was running late, because he sure was. By the time he left the livery, it was close to one-thirty. He expected even after the liveryman took his cut, the sale of the two horses and the dead men's gear would provide Jill more than two hundred dollars. That would make for a nice little nest egg.

It was a surprise to find the money on Jeets. Billy figured all the robbers got from the train, including what was in the strong box and what they took from the passengers, couldn't have totaled more than five hundred dollars. He doubted the leader would be willing to split it fifty-fifty, but if he was, even with half going to each man, it would have only come to maybe two-fifty apiece. How could Jeets Duvall have given Leo Springer three hundred and still have forty-three dollars in his pocket? It didn't make sense. Billy doubted Jeets's cowboying pay would make up the difference, but it was clear he'd gotten the money somewhere.

By the time Billy got to the station, the train had arrived, and with the help of one of the train crew, Mr. Somerhill was loading the casket containing Bernard Simms into his wagon.

A woman dressed in black stood beside the hearse watching. Billy assumed this to be the widow.

"Pardon me, ma'am," he asked. "Are you, by chance, Mrs. Simms?"

The woman turned toward Billy and nodded. "I am." She

was a matronly woman, in her late forties or early fifties. Her eyes were dry as she watched them load the body of her husband, but they were ringed in red from the tears she'd shed over the course of the last three days.

Billy took off his hat. "My name is Billy Young. I was on the train with your husband at the time of the robbery."

"Yes," she said. "Sheriff Linford was just here, and he mentioned you. He tells me your brother was also murdered, and you have extracted justice from two of the killers."

"Well, I've taken their lives, ma'am."

"That's as close to justice as we come on this earth, Mr. Young. The sheriff says you are searching for the third man as well."

"Yes, but I'm stumped as to where to look. I believe his name is Zeke Blood. Is that a name familiar to you?"

"No," she said. "I'm sorry, but it's not."

"I doubted it would be. It may take me a while, but sooner or later I'll find him. I don't plan to quit until I do." He lifted the watch and chain from his pocket. "One of the killers had this on him, ma'am. I recognized it as belonging to your husband."

He held it out, and the woman removed a black glove and took the watch from his palm. She stared at it for a moment, then clutched it to her breast and lowered her head.

Billy shoved his hands into his pockets and said nothing.

After a moment, the woman pulled a lace-trimmed handkerchief from her sleeve and daubed her eyes. "I'm sorry," she said. "I thought I was all cried out, but it seems I was mistaken."

"It's all right, ma'am. I understand. It's a hard thing."

"Did he die well, young man?" she asked.

At first Billy didn't know what she meant, but then he understood. "Yes." His answer was automatic. In truth, Billy had no real memory of how Bernard Simms had died. He did recall that Simms was the first man shot after the killers lined

91

everyone up. It was the leader, Blood, who killed him before anyone realized it was going to happen. "He died bravely," Billy added. "And it was fast. He felt no pain, I'm sure."

"I'm glad to hear that," the woman said. "Bernard wasn't a brave man by nature. He was a good man, a very good man, but he was—" She seemed to search for a word. "—meek, I guess you might say."

"He showed no meekness that day, ma'am. None at all."

"It's ironic," she said, "that he should be killed in this senseless robbery. He was running from something, you know."

"Ma'am?"

"Yes, he was trying to get away from something here that had him frightened, and what should happen but through stupid bad luck, he should fall into a situation even more terrifying than anything he might have encountered here in Probity."

"Why was he running?" Billy asked.

"I don't know. He wouldn't explain to me what it was, but it was clear he felt threatened. He was on his way to Miles City. Once he was settled in, he was going to send for me. He said he wanted to leave this country for good." She looked down at the watch in her hand. "I gave this to him on the day we were married. It's a fine watch."

"Yes," Billy agreed, "it's a beauty."

She smiled. "We couldn't afford it, of course. We were newlyweds just starting out, but I wanted to give him something nice."

Because their attention was focused on the elaborately etched case of the watch the woman held, they didn't notice the approach of Somerhill, the mortician. "Excuse me, Mrs. Simms," he said, doffing his hat, "but I am finished here, and I wanted to let you know everything is prepared for the services tomorrow."

"Thank you, sir."

"I also want you to know I checked the body, and Mr. Simms looks very peaceful. Very peaceful, indeed. I'm sure you will be most pleased."

"Yes."

"By the way," said Somerhill, "Mr. Teasdale, my counterpart in Casper, sent along a note explaining that he had found this tucked into the lining of your husband's suit coat." He handed her a small notebook. "He said it was all that was on the body."

"Thank you again, Mr. Somerhill. You've been most kind. I will see you tomorrow."

The man smiled and said, "Madam." He replaced his hat. "Young man." And he returned to his hearse.

The woman thumbed the pages of the notebook she held. The pages were all lined, but only the first twenty-five or so contained any markings, and the markings were unlike anything Billy had ever seen.

"What is it?" he asked.

"Oh, nothing, really. Just one of my husband's tablets. He has—*had* hundreds of them. Literally hundreds. He keeps them stored in his office. He seldom carries one around when he's not working." She raised her head and gave Billy a misty look. Her tears had stopped, but her eyes remained moist. "I keep slipping back into the present tense, don't I? It's hard to believe he's gone." She swallowed and said, "I must remember to speak in the past tense. How long does it take, I wonder, for that to come of its own accord?"

Billy knew her question was not directed at him.

After a bit he asked, "May I see it?" He indicated the notebook. She handed it to him, and he looked at all the odd scribblings it contained. For all Billy could make of it, these swirls, lines, and dots might as well have been Egyptian hieroglyphics. "What sort of employment did your husband have, Mrs. Simms?"

"He was a stenographer, a court reporter. He reported the proceedings at trials and in depositions. He was very proficient. He could write words as fast as they were spoken. It was amazing."

He held the tablet opened to the first page and lifted it for her to see. "Is this how he wrote it," Billy asked, "with marks like these?"

"Yes," the woman answered, "it's called Pitman shorthand. Bernard was in school in Chicago learning the skill when we met and married."

"Are you able to read it?" Billy asked.

"Oh, my, no, not a word. Bernard was the only one around here who could read Pitman. The next closest court stenographer would be in Casper."

"Why would you suppose your husband would keep this particular notebook with him when he kept all the others back in his office?"

The woman's eyes narrowed as she gave the question some thought. Then she shook her head and said, "I can't imagine." She paused, started to say more, but stopped herself again.

"What is it?"

"I was going to say it was not like Bernard. He was a meticulous man, particularly as it pertained to his work. Forgetting to file away a set of notes would not be like him, not at all."

"Mr. Somerhill did say it was found in the lining of his coat. It could be the inside of his pocket was torn and the notebook fell through into the lining."

"Yes," Mrs. Simms allowed, "I suppose that's possible."

"You mentioned he was upset. Do you have any idea what was bothering him?"

The woman's lips pursed together, and she turned and crossed the platform to a bench set against the outside wall of the station. Billy followed, and they both sat down. "In many

94

ways, Mr. Young, my husband was a very fanciful man." She spoke without facing Billy. Instead, she watched the white steam huff around the locomotive that had brought her husband's body home. "He was even a Romantic, you might say. We were never blessed with children, and—well, it seems a little ludicrous to say this sort of thing in the cold light of day, I suppose, but he tended to idolize our life together. He placed our marriage on a pedestal. He tried his best to protect it and me from the harsh realities of everyday life. As a consequence, he told me little or nothing about his work or his dealings outside our home."

"So you knew nothing of what might have been troubling him?"

"I wouldn't say I knew nothing. Bernard is—was the fanciful one, Mr. Young. I am not. After Bernard became so upset and left the other afternoon in such a rush, I went to his office and checked his appointment book to see if there might be some indication there of what was bothering him so."

"Did you find anything?"

"Nothing of certainty, but Bernard was late coming home the evening before he left. It was almost midnight. That was when I first noticed his agitation. I'm sure he got no sleep that night at all. He was tossing and turning, so neither did I. The next day after he left and I checked his appointment book, I found he had scheduled a reporting assignment for the evening before. He hadn't noted what sort of an assignment, only the time it was to begin—ten o'clock. An odd hour."

"Why's that?"

"Well, I'm certain there are no court proceedings set at that time, and I doubt anyone would be providing a deposition that needed to be reported verbatim at such an hour."

"It wouldn't seem likely, I don't suppose."

"Another odd thing occurred the next morning—very early

the next morning."

"What was that?"

"A man came by our house to speak with Bernard. Whatever conversation they had, though, was brief, but it was after that conversation that Bernard became most upset. He told me he had to leave, and he would send for me. Of course, I tried to get him to explain what was happening, but he wouldn't. He said not telling me was for my own good."

"Who was it who came by that morning?" Billy asked.

"Caldwell Unger," Mrs. Simms answered. "And, according to my husband's appointment book, it was Caldwell Unger who had hired his services for the evening before."

Before Billy left Mrs. Simms, he asked if he might hang on to her husband's notebook for a while. She seemed confused as to why he would want it, but even when he was unable to provide her with a logical explanation, she still agreed he could take it along.

Billy knew the reason he could not provide a logical explanation was that there was no logic involved, only curiosity. It seemed a peculiar coincidence that two men would spend an evening together and the next day one of those men would flee town in a panic, and before the sun had set, they both were dead. And even though there was no obvious connection between the tablet and those events, Billy thought the shorthand notes might provide a clue as to what had happened.

Of course, there was no reason to believe any of this had anything to do with the train robbery, but Billy thought it was strange enough that it deserved to be looked into, and, besides, since he had no idea where to begin his search for Zeke Blood, he had nothing better to do.

He went into the depot and purchased a ticket for the afternoon train to Casper—the same departure time Bernard

Simms had booked three days before—then went next door to
the telegraph office and sent a wire to Hugo Dorling, asking
Hugo to meet him at the Casper depot. Hugo knew everyone in
town with any official or professional status, and Billy requested
Hugo bring along the local court reporter.

After sending the telegram, Billy had forty minutes to kill
before the westbound train arrived and at least an hour before it
departed. In that time he returned to the livery stable to board
Badger for the night.

"I'll pay you in advance," Billy told the liveryman. "I expect
to be back by early tomorrow afternoon."

"All right, young fella, I'll take good care of 'im."

Billy gave the gray's rump a smack as the man led the horse
to a stall. "Say," Billy called out, "where do you suppose a man
could buy some cartridges around here?"

"Couple of places. There's Otto's, the gun shop on the far
end of First Street by the old stage depot. He don't have too
much, though. Mostly Otto just works on guns, but he does
keep a supply of the more common stuff, forty-four-forties and
some shotgun shells, twelve gauge, mostly, maybe some tens. If
you're not looking for something standard like that, your best
bet'd be McConners' General Store, right on Center. John Mc-
Conners stocks about anything you might ever need."

"Obliged," Billy said, and he left the livery and headed the
two blocks over to Center Street.

Billy knew Bernard Simms encountered something or
someone the night before the robbery that frightened him
enough he wanted to leave town in a hurry, and since Simms
had spent some time with Caldwell Unger during the previous
evening, Billy wondered if Unger's behavior the next day had
been strange as well. He needed to visit with someone who had
been with him, but since Unger's wife was now with her sister
in Nebraska, Billy would have to locate some other person

who'd seen Unger on that last day.

McConners' General Store was a well-stocked and well-tended establishment filled with the aroma of freshly ground coffee, unsmoked tobacco, peppermint candy, and a hundred other smells that all mixed together in a pleasant way. A large Ben Franklin surrounded by a half dozen chairs was in the center of the room. Billy suspected on cold winter days those chairs were occupied by philosophers and political pundits, but now they sat empty. A long counter ran the length of the building. Behind the counter was a thin, balding man with sleeve garters, spectacles, and the stub of a pencil tucked behind his right ear.

"Afternoon, young sir," the man said with a cordial smile as Billy approached.

"Afternoon. Are you Mr. McConners?" Billy asked.

"I am. John McConners." The storekeeper extended his hand over the counter, and Billy gave it a shake.

"Billy Young. I'm from around Casper. Got a place over there."

"Welcome to Probity. What can I do for you?"

"I was wondering if Mr. Caldwell Unger might have come into your store here the morning of his accident to buy some ammunition for his rifle. I figure he had to have either come in here or over to the gun shop, one or the other."

The man rubbed his chin. "No, Mrs. Unger always does the shopping, but Cal would drop by from time to time, usually for pipe tobacco. He had a fine collection of meerschaums and enjoyed a good tobacco. I don't remember him coming in on that day, though."

"Well, if he was looking for ammunition, it must've been the gun shop he went to after all," Billy said, "because I'd expect if he came in, you would remember it. He would've been purchasing fifty-six-caliber rimfires for his Spencer. I doubt it's a thing you sell much of these days."

McConners laughed and agreed, "No, we sure don't." He walked down the counter a ways and came through a swinging gate into the main area of his store. "If you'll hold on just a second, though, I'll check and see." He crossed the room to a far wall, ran his finger along a line of boxes, and said, "Well, you know, by golly, he might've come in at that. We had us four boxes of fifty-six rimfires last week, and now we only have three. But I'm sure I didn't wait on him. Like you said, I'd've remembered selling a box of them big rimfires." He turned and walked to a door in the back, opened it, and called, "Hey, son, come out here, would you?"

A boy of sixteen or seventeen entered the room. It was the same adolescent who had given Billy directions to the sheriff's office earlier. Mr. McConners placed a hand on the boy's shoulder. "This fella's my son. He sometimes waits on customers, too." He looked down at the boy and asked, "Micah, do you remember selling a box of fifty-six-caliber rimfires to Mr. Unger the other day—the day of his unfortunate accident?"

The boy thought for a second and said, "No, sir, not to Mr. Unger, but I did sell a box to a couple of other men."

"A couple of other men?" asked Billy. "Do you know their names?"

Micah shook his head. "Nope, never saw them before. I did see one of them since, though."

Billy felt his eyebrows lift. "You did? When?"

"This morning. He was that little fella you had slung over the back of a horse."

CHAPTER TEN

Hugo Dorling and a young man dressed in a baseball uniform met Billy at the Casper train depot.

"Howdy, Billy," Hugo called out as Billy stepped down from the passenger car. The old lawman hustled over to Billy, and the ballplayer came up behind. "This here's Walter P. Cosgrove," Hugo said. "He's one of them fast writers that reports all the trials for Judge Bishop over at the District Court."

Cosgrove and Billy shook hands. "Mr. Cosgrove," Billy said, "nice to meet you."

"Just call me Walt." He was only a couple of years older than Billy.

"All right. Walt it is."

The man was large—not so large as Fritz Gruber, but he was at least four inches taller than Billy and must have outweighed him by at least twenty-five pounds. He was put together like an athlete, with wide shoulders and narrow hips, and his broad, friendly face held a stubby little nose in its center that was as pugged as a shoat's.

Hugo gave the young man a slap on the back. "Walt here's the first baseman for the Casper Red Stockin's. I yanked him off the diamond right after their game today so's we could meet you here at the station like you asked in your telegram."

"Glad you could come, Walt," Billy said.

Walt lifted his cap and ran his fingers through a shock of coarse red hair. "No problem," he said, "but what's this all about, anyway?"

"To be honest," answered Billy, "I'm not sure exactly. Do you know another fella in your profession by the name of Bernard Simms?"

"Sure do. He lives over in Probity."

"Well, sir, that's right. At least he did. I'm sorry to tell you, but Bernard Simms is dead. He was one of the men who was murdered along with my brother in the train robbery the other day."

The baseball player's freckled face blanched. "Murdered?" He shoved the ball cap back on his head. "Mr. Simms is dead? Why, that's awful."

Billy dug into his pocket and pulled out the notebook. "This tablet was found on his body. It has some writing in it, and I expect you're the only one around here who can read what it says."

Walter Cosgrove took the tablet out of Billy's hand and flipped through it. "Yep," he said, "it looks to be written in Pitman. Of course, everyone has his own style. Sometimes no one can read a reporter's notes but the fella who wrote them." He gave a sheepish grin. "And sometimes even he can't read 'em." He glanced again at the tablet. "But I expect I could read this, if I was given a little time."

"What're you gettin' at, Billy?" Hugo asked.

"I'm hoping whatever's written in there'll shed some light on the train robbery and maybe another man's death that happened in Probity on the same day." He looked again toward Walter Cosgrove. "Do you think you could write it down for me in a—what is it you fellas call those things?"

"A transcript?"

"Right. Do you think you could make up one of those transcripts for me? I'd be glad to pay you, of course."

"I expect I could. When would you need it?"

"Well, as soon as you could get it."

Walt did a quick count of the number of pages in the tablet with writing. "How about by noon tomorrow? Would that be soon enough?"

"I'll be needing to catch the eleven-thirty eastbound. Do you think you could have it a little before then?"

"Sure. I'll try to have it for you by eleven."

"That's fine." Billy dug into his pocket, pulled out a Double Eagle, and offered it to the man.

"Hang on to your money until we see what I can come up with." He tapped an index finger to the bill of his cap and turned to leave. "Come by my offices tomorrow morning."

"I sure will," Billy said. "And thanks a lot."

When Walt was gone, Billy said, "He seems to be a likeable fella."

"He does, don't he?" Hugo agreed. "And I tell ya, he is one baseball-playin' son of a bitch. So far this season the boy's hittin' better than four hundred for the Stockin's."

"Is that so?" Billy said. "Well, let's hope he's as good at reading gibberish as he is at swinging a bat. Come on, I'll buy you a steak and a beer, and then I'm getting a room over at the Wentworth. I've hardly slept a wink since night before last."

Billy and Hugo were slow eating their supper. By the time they had put away a couple of hefty porterhouses, they were the only ones left in the small café.

"So, I left the general store and went back to the sheriff's office." Billy took a sip from his fourth mug of beer. "I told Sheriff Linford about two of the men from the train robbery buying the shells for the Spencer the morning of Unger's death." It had taken the entire meal for Billy to relate all the events of the previous three days.

"What did the sheriff have to say about that?" Hugo asked.

"Not much to say, I guess. We decided there wasn't anything

to do since both men were already dead. I told him about Simms's notebook, and that I was bringing it over here to Casper to have the local court reporter see if he could make anything of it." He gave a shrug. "We just left it at that."

"Damn, boy," Hugo observed, "sounds like you've had yourself quite the adventure in the last few days." The lawman chuckled as he twisted up a smoke. "Care for an after-supper shuck?" he asked.

Billy had never taken to tobacco. It made him dizzy and left a foul taste in his mouth, but he thought a little smoke right now might perk him up some. He could use perking up. His eyelids felt like someone had tied a couple of fishing weights to them. "Sure," he said, "I don't mind if I do, but I'm embarrassed to admit I never learned how to roll 'em up."

"Here, take this one." Hugo handed the one he'd just made to Billy, peeled off another paper, and rolled a second for himself. He struck a light, touched it to both cigarettes, and dropped the match onto his plate, where it fizzled in a puddle of steak juice.

"I've had some adventures myself since you've been gone."

"How's that?" Billy asked.

"We discovered our dead Indian agent weren't killed by a couple of reservation bucks after all."

"I thought you found the knife that was the murder weapon. Didn't it carry Arapaho markings?"

"We did, and it did, but it turns out the killer ain't an Indian. He's a Baptist deacon by the name of Hiram Sanders. It seems the agent became a little too friendly with Mrs. Sanders, and the deacon took offense."

"Have you arrested him?"

"Can't find the sneaky bastard, leastwise I ain't found him yet, but I know he's holed up here in town somewhere, and it's only a matter of time before I get him. He used the Arapaho knife on the agent then planted the damned thing in the alley so we'd find it. I reckon the lesson there is things ain't always what they seem."

Billy inhaled smoke from the cigarette the way he'd seen Hugo and other full-time smokers do. He held it for a bit then blew it out with a cough. He was still trying to fight off the cough when he felt his head begin to swim. "Damn," he said, looking down at the cigarette, "these things'll make you drunk."

Hugo sent Billy a quick frown that Billy figured was disgust at his inability to handle a little smoke without getting light-headed.

"Tell me again what it is you hope to get outta them hen scratchin's you turned over to young Walter," Hugo said.

"I don't know. Something happened that night, and it could be the writing in the tablet will explain it."

"I expect it *will* explain it," Hugo said in a matter-of-fact tone. "Maybe not explain it all, but some."

That perked Billy up in a way the cigarette had not. "Why do you say that?" he asked.

" 'Cause I don't believe a man as particular as you say this Simms fella was is ever gonna have a hole in his pocket. That's why. It's as simple as that. I might have a hole in my pocket, and you might, too, but from the sounds of it, that fella ain't. Now, if he ain't gonna have a hole in his pocket, it means he stuck the notebook into the lining of his suit on purpose, and if he goes to that much trouble, it stands to figure there's some-thin' written on it he don't want just anybody to see, even if they ain't able to read what's writ there without goin' to some effort."

"You could be right."

"You can bet on it."

"Well, that's encouraging."

"What it may not do is get you any closer to Mr. Blood, and

that's what you want, ain't it?"

Billy felt the muscles in his jaw tighten. "When it comes down to it, that's all I want. But I know there's a connection. There has to be. Why else would Jeets Duvall and Noah Baxter be buying rounds for a Spencer repeating rifle?"

"Could be they owned one, too," Hugo suggested.

"Not likely."

"No," the lawman agreed, "I reckon not."

Billy took a last draw of the cigarette and snuffed it into his plate. His fatigue was soaking into him as he sat and watched the last stream of smoke rise from the butt.

"Is there somethin' else botherin' you, kid?" Hugo asked. "You seem pensive."

Billy looked up and smiled. "Pensive? Nice word, Hugo."

"Hell, boy, I'm an educated fella. I'll have you know I finished the third grade with the highest possible marks."

Billy's smile turned to a laugh, but as fast as they had come, the smile and laughter were gone and his weariness settled back in.

"What's on your mind, there, Billy-boy?"

Billy lifted his gaze to Hugo, and after a bit he said, "You know, Hugo, Poppa used to tell me and Frank that any man who pays attention to the world around him'll always be able to recognize right from wrong. It's an easy thing, he said, if you just pay attention."

Hugo nodded. "Your pa was a good man. Probably the best friend I ever had."

"I believed him, too," Billy said, "a man will know what's right and what's wrong. I still believe it, I guess . . . mostly."

They sat for a while sipping their beer, not talking. It was not an awkward silence, but it did lay heavy on the table. It was Hugo who broke it. "It's the killin', ain't it, boy?"

Billy gave the older man a quick nod. "But it's not the doing it that's bothering me. It appears I can do it easy enough."

"What then?"

"It's how the doing it makes me feel." He took in a deep breath and slowly let it go. "I didn't have to hang Jeets Duvall, Hugo. I had him caught. He was beat. I could've taken him into Probity and turned him over to the law, but I didn't do it."

"How come?"

"Because I wanted to kill him. I killed him in that dark cabin because I figured he deserved it, and I wanted to be the one to do it. I didn't even give the idea of taking him back any consideration at all." He swallowed and looked down at the spent cigarette on his plate. "At first I thought if I killed these fellas it would fill up some empty place I had after Frank was murdered. When I killed Noah Baxter and that spot wasn't filled, I thought, well, all right, okay, after I kill Jeets Duvall, it will be. But when I killed Jeets, it still wasn't full."

"Could be," Hugo said, "it's a spot that ain't never gonna fill up."

"I've decided that's probably the truth, but it doesn't change anything. I'm going to hunt the last man down, too, and when I find him, I'm not going to take him to the law, either. I'm going to kill him just as dead as I killed those other two. The only difference is this time I won't be doing it with the hope it might replace something I've lost."

"Why will you be doin' it?" Hugo asked.

Billy started to answer but stopped himself. "I don't know," he finally said.

Hugo sat up straight in his chair and leaned forward right into Billy's face. "Bull shit," he said. "You know why you're gonna kill him. You're just ashamed to tell it."

Billy felt his eyes widen. It was true, Billy did know, and he was ashamed.

"You're goin' after that fella, Blood," Hugo continued, "and when you find him, you're gonna kill him, and you're right when you say you ain't doin' it to fill some empty spot caused by the grief of losin' your brother. You ain't doin' it for justice, neither, Billy Young. These're men who done robbed a train, but even with that, they decided outta pure meanness, I reckon, to murder everyone in sight. The reason you want to kill the leader of the group that'd do somethin' like that is because killin' him'll give you pleasure, just like killin' them others already gave you pleasure. You're doin' it for that reason and that reason alone. Maybe it won't fill the empty spot you have, but it *will* give you pleasure." Hugo leaned back in his chair. "Now, I'm sure that ain't what your pa, the good Joshua Young, would call right, but it's the truth. I know it and you know it, too."

Billy nodded. "It is the truth," he allowed. "It is." He dropped his head, and for the first time in at least ten years he thought he was going to cry. He didn't cry at the graves of his parents, nor did he cry when he buried Frank. But sitting there in that small café with Hugo Dorling, he had to bite his lip and dig his nails into the meat of his palms to keep the tears at bay.

After a bit he said in a hoarse voice, "Folks around here already think I'm crazy."

"You ain't crazy, boy."

With that his head came up, and it was Billy who leaned across the table. "Sane men kill to protect themselves or to protect their families," he said. "Sane men kill to enforce the law. Hell, Hugo, sane men might even kill for revenge. But it's the crazy ones who kill for pleasure, even if the only ones they ever kill are deserving. If they get pleasure from the deed, killing is in their blood, and they're crazy." He leaned back into his chair and looked away from the older man. His exhaustion now was as deep as his soul. "It's a good thing Poppa's not around to see what has happened to his sons. One shot down and the other—" His voice trailed off.

"Billy," Hugo said, "you listen to me. The world ain't a simple place. Your pa was a good man, but he was able to see things as clear as he did because he was lucky enough to always be standin' in the light. That's just the way things work out sometimes. Some folks is lucky and some ain't. Some folks, boy, get to spend their whole damned lives standin' in the warm sunshine. But there's others—me, for instance, and you—who, because of the sorta things that gets tossed our way, we have to sometimes go down into dark places. And down in them dark places, it ain't so easy to see." He let out a long, slow breath. Now Hugo, too, seemed exhausted, and not just from the events of the previous few days. Hugo's exhaustion seemed to stretch further back.

He cleared his throat and added, "The colors ain't so bright down in them dark places, Billy. Fact is, what little that can be seen down there mostly looks pretty damned gray."

Hugo stopped talking and swirled the last slosh of beer left in his mug. He watched the suds spin for a bit then looked again at Billy.

Billy could tell there was more the old lawman wished he could say, but for whatever reason, he offered nothing more.

CHAPTER ELEVEN

Billy took a room at the Wentworth Hotel and slept a deep, dreamless sleep. He woke late, washed up, and went down to the restaurant for a breakfast of gravy and biscuits. When he finished, he stepped outside for a breath of air.

It was still more than an hour before he was to pick up the transcript from Walter Cosgrove, and he was pondering how to fill that time when Hugo Dorling walked up.

"Have a good sleep, Billy?" Hugo asked.

"I did, and I needed it. I feel better. Maybe not good," he added, "but I do feel better."

The older man smiled and nodded.

Billy rubbed a hand across his jaw. "I was thinking I might head over to the barber's for a shave." It had been four days since he'd last shaved, and although his beard was not a fast grower, he was showing signs of stubble. "You're looking pretty scruffy yourself, there, Hugo. Care to come along?"

"I don't never pay for shaves," the thrifty deputy replied, stroking a palm along his own cheek. "Seems a waste of money."

"Come on," said Billy, "it'll be my treat."

Hugo pulled out his watch and checked the time. "I'm s'posed to see a fella sometime this mornin' who I figure'll give me a lead on where I can locate my murderin' deacon." He snapped the watch closed and slipped it back into the small watch pocket of his jeans. "But I reckon I've got enough time before then to let you waste your money."

On the way down a side street to the barbershop, they had to pass the office of Walter Cosgrove. Beside the court reporter's front door hung a sign that read:

Walter P. Cosgrove
——Stenographer——

Verbatim Reporting
of
Trials, Depositions,
and
Hearings of Every Kind

"Let's go in and see how Walt's coming with the transcript he's making," Billy said.

They pushed open the door to see the young court reporter sitting in his shirt sleeves at a huge oak desk. Bernard Simms's notebook was opened and lying on the desktop next to an ornately decorated typing machine. The typewriter was inlaid with mother of pearl, painted roses, and gold scrollwork. The keyboard was made up of two rows of square-topped keys. Across the front of the machine, in fancy script, was written the word "Crandall."

Walt offered them his quick smile. "Morning, gents." He checked the wall clock. "You're a bit early, I believe."

"We're not here to rush you," Billy said. "We were just passing by and thought we might see how things were going."

"Things are going well," said Walter. "Mr. Simms had a fine hand—easy to read."

He rolled three sheets of paper from his typewriter. Two were ordinary white sheets, and sandwiched between these was a sheet of black. Both white sheets contained printing from top to bottom, and Walt turned the top sheet over and placed it onto a stack to the right of the typing machine. He then did the same with the other white sheet, placing it on a stack to the left. The black sheet he placed inside a drawer.

"I'm making an original and one copy for you, Mr. Young. I figured one copy'd be enough."

"Sure, that'll be fine."

Walt took a new sheet of black paper from another drawer and inserted it between two fresh sheets of white. "For a transcript," Walter explained, "I like to use a piece of carbon only once. It keeps the copy nice and sharp." He nodded toward the drawer full of used sheets of carbon paper. "I save 'em, though, to use later. They're still plenty good enough for letters and ordering supplies and that sort of thing."

He rolled the three fresh sheets of paper into his typewriter.

Billy was tempted to pick up one of the stacks and start to read but decided he should wait until the job was complete. He was curious, though, as to what they contained.

"Are Mr. Simms's notes of interest?" Billy couldn't help but ask.

Walt leaned back in his chair. "Well, sir," he said, "they are. This is not a court hearing, nor a deposition. It's a bunch of men sitting in a room talking, and it's clear to me the reporting of it was being done on the sly."

"Beg pardon?" Hugo said.

Walt nodded toward the tablet. "Mr. Simms was making a record of these men's conversation, but the men having the conversation were not aware of his presence."

"How can you know that?" asked Billy.

The stenographer chuckled. "Because men do not say the sorts of things these fellas were saying if they know someone's writing it all down. I expect Mr. Simms was in an adjacent room with the door ajar, or perhaps outside a window eavesdropping."

"Who are the men?" Hugo asked.

"Simms only used initials to designate the speakers, but occasionally one of them would call another by name. Even without that, though, it wouldn't be hard to figure out who these fellas are just by the things they're saying. Also, I'm familiar with the ranchers of the larger spreads in the Probity area. That's who these fellas are. I'll note at the end of the transcript who each of the initials stands for. It's clear Caldwell Unger is present. Caldwell's a lawyer from over that way. He and I have worked together a few times on different cases."

"What sorts of things were they discussing?" asked Billy.

Walt shrugged. "It sounds to me like there was less discussing going on than there was conspiring." Again he checked the clock. "But rather than me taking the time to tell you about it, Billy, why don't you give me another, say, thirty minutes or so, and you can read it for yourself."

"All right, Walter, that sounds fair to me. We were headed to the barber's anyway. Come along, Hugo. You're looking scruffier by the second."

After their shaves, Hugo and Billy stepped from the barbershop and made their way back to Walter's office. It felt good to Billy to have the stubble scraped from his face, but Hugo would not stop complaining that the barber had trimmed his mustache too short.

He rubbed the fingers of both hands across his upper lip. "I knew I shoulda never let that son of a bitch come near my handsome mustaches with them damned scissors. He oughta be a butcher, not a barber."

Unfortunately, Billy thought, it had not been necessary for the barber to trim Billy's own skimpy mustache, and to Hugo's credit, the old deputy did not point that out.

From the time they left for their shaves until they returned, it had been a little over forty minutes. "I expect we've given Walt enough time to finish up," Billy said as he pushed open the office door.

"It's amazin' to me," said Hugo, "how them stenographer fellas can write as fast as they do in the first—" What they saw when they stepped into the office caused the words to catch in Hugo's throat. After a bit he croaked out, "My Lord, look at this place."

The office was in a shambles. Hat trees and chairs were overturned. Pictures and Walter's diploma were knocked from the walls. The typewriter was twisted and broken on the floor.

Billy crossed to a half-opened door on the far wall. The door led into a storage room.

"What the devil happened here?" Hugo asked.

"I'm not sure," answered Billy, "but it looks like there was one hell of a fight."

A door in the rear of the storage room gaped open, and Billy ran to take a look. This door led into an alley, but there was nothing there to see.

"Say, Billy," Hugo called, "come back in here and take a look at this."

Billy returned, and Hugo pointed to a dozen or so red spots that ran in a line along the floor. Billy bent for a closer look. "Blood," he said. "And it leads to the back alley. Whoever it was must've taken Walt out that way."

Hugo went back into the front office, and Billy followed. "It looks like young Walter put up a damned fine fight," Hugo said. "I've seen him get into scrapes out on the ball field, and I guarantee you it'd take at least four strong men to take Walter Cosgrove someplace he didn't wanna go."

Billy scanned the desktop and the debris that littered the floor. "They took the transcript, too," he said.

Hugo looked around. "Well, I'll be damned. So they did."

"I wish I'd taken what he'd already typed with me when we went for our shaves."

"Hell, Billy, there was no way for us to know somethin' like this'd happen."

Billy watched as Hugo went to the front door and called out to a boy rolling a hoop down the street. "You, there, boy, get to Sheriff Jarrell's office and tell him we need him over here right away."

The kid stopped and stared. "What's goin' on, mister?"

"Jus' do as you're told before I come out there and box your ears."

Billy recalled from his own childhood that Hugo Dorling was never one to show a lot of patience toward kids.

"They wanted the transcript, Hugo," Billy said. "That's what this is all about."

"Could be you're right," Hugo allowed, "but who-all knew we were even askin' Walt to make one?"

Billy thought about it for a second. "Well, I told the sheriff over in Probity, and, of course, Mrs. Simms when I got the tablet from her in the first place. I mentioned it to Jill Springer. When I was waiting for the train, I stopped by the boarding house to tell her I was coming to Casper."

"Well, however it happened, it's clear knowledge of a transcript bein' made got to the wrong set of ears."

Billy felt his insides shudder. His asking Walter Cosgrove to transcribe those notes at least brought the young stenographer a beating, and, Billy hated to admit, maybe something worse.

"Goddamn it," Billy shouted, smashing his fist onto the top of Walter's desk. "Who are these people, and what the hell is going on here?"

Hugo righted one of the office chairs and took a seat. "It's a hard one to figure. That's for sure."

"The transcript," Billy said. "If we only had the Goddamned—" Billy had a thought. "Wait a minute, Hugo. Maybe—"

Billy opened the desk drawer that held Walt's used carbon paper and took out the top sheet. The paper was carbonized on one side. The other side was clean, dark, and smooth. There were marks on both sides of the paper where the type bars had struck. Billy lifted the sheet to the light. Yes, he believed with some effort he could make out most of the words. Some were more distinct than others. Some were not decipherable at all, but at least it was something.

Billy dug the top twenty sheets of carbon paper from the drawer. There had been, maybe, ten pages completed when Billy and Hugo had left for the barbershop, so by taking twice that many, he was confident he'd collected all the sheets of carbon Walt had used to produce the Simms transcript. He folded the pages and shoved them into his shirt.

Billy checked the clock. "Hugo," he said, "would you mind waiting here for the sheriff? I've got to catch my train."

"Be glad to, son. You go ahead."

"You can reach me at Mrs. Jordan's Boarding House in Probity. If anything turns up on Walt, send me a telegram."

"I'll do 'er," Hugo said. "You can betcher life I will."

For once the eastbound arrived in Probity on time and pulled into the station right at one-seventeen.

As the train huffed to a stop, Billy jumped onto the platform and ran the three blocks to Mrs. Jordan's Boarding House, where he took lodging for the night.

"This'll be fine," Billy said to the widow when she showed him to his room.

"Supper's at six this evening," Mrs. Jordan said. "Breakfast is served at seven in the morning." The woman turned to leave. "I hope you're comfortable, Mr. Young. If you need anything,

please don't hesitate to either let me or one of my girls know."
Mrs. Jordan was a pretty woman with a trim figure, who looked
to be maybe fifteen years older than Billy.

"Yes, ma'am. Before you go, though, I was wondering, would
it be possible to see Jill Springer?"

"Yes, of course. Her morning chores're finished, and she'll be
off work until it's time to serve supper. I'll check to see if she's
in her room. If she is, I'll send her in." Again the widow turned
to leave, but she stopped herself short. "You understand, young
man, I expect you to leave your room door open."

"What? Oh, yes, ma'am. Absolutely. That is not a problem.
Not a problem at all. We sure will." Billy was embarrassed by
what Mrs. Jordan implied, but as she turned to leave, Billy saw
the edges of her hazel eyes crinkle into a hint of a smile.

As soon as she was gone, Billy pulled the carbons from his
shirt and stacked them on a table next to the room's window.
He was tempted to try to read them on the train, but the car
was crowded, and he hadn't wanted to draw attention. Now,
though, he dug down to the bottom of the stack to where he
presumed the first page of the transcript would be. He pulled it
out and lifted it to the light.

He tried to focus his eyes onto what he held, and once he
did, he felt his heart skitter. There were markings on the paper,
but they were impossible to read. It was nothing more than a
series of blurred, indecipherable lines, one line beneath the
other, all the way to the bottom of the page.

He picked up the next one. It was the same, and so was the
one after that. Billy's throat closed as he made a grab for the
fourth. It, to his relief, was better. It was difficult, but he could
just make out some individual letters. Billy tried to swallow
away the knot around his Adam's apple. The first three sheets
must have been the ones Walt had used more than once, and
each time he used them, the vowels and consonants piled onto

one another, each striking over the top of the one that had come before.

"Damn," Billy said aloud. His voice was coarse, and he inhaled a deep breath in an effort to settle himself down.

The table where he sat held a drawer, and he opened it to find a stack of writing paper and a half-dozen graphite pencils. He pulled out the paper and a pencil, lifted the carbon and placed it flush against the window pane. The light passing through helped to make out the letters, but still it was not an easy chore.

This page was, though, Billy decided, the first carbon from Bernard Simms's transcript. As Billy struggled to read the words, he wrote them onto the paper he had taken from the drawer. It took a while for him to decipher the first line, but he could feel his excitement rise as he printed the words across the page.

CU: Sit down, gentlemen. Would anyone care for a drink?

CHAPTER TWELVE

Billy had been working less than ten minutes when there was a gentle rapping at his door.

"Come in," he called without turning around. He was staring into the dim markings of the carbon paper. "Is that you, Jill?"

"Yes."

He took the paper away from the window. "You better leave the door open," he said as he turned around. "Mrs. Jordan already warned me she—" He stopped in mid-sentence because the sense of whatever it was he was about to say had left him. The reason for that, he knew, was the beauty of this girl who stood in the center of his room. "My God, Jill, you look—" Again, he lost what he was trying to say.

Jill smiled and ran her hands down the front of her starched dress. "Mrs. Jordan gave me this gingham of hers. She's a very kind person, Mrs. Jordan is."

"Yes," Billy agreed, "she is. You, er, uh—" He coughed but was able to sputter out, "—look wonderful." And she did. Of course, the only time Billy had ever seen her she had been at her worst, but that was a mere twenty-two hours before, and he couldn't believe the difference. Marks were still visible on her face, and there was still a little swelling, but as she stood before him now, Jill Springer looked—"Wonderful," Billy repeated.

The young girl smiled and stared down at her hands. "How was your trip to Casper?"

Her question brought Billy back to the present. "It was not

118

good," he answered. "Not good at all." He gave her a quick rundown of events, and Jill listened without speaking. When he was finished, he led her to the table beside the window.

"I haven't deciphered too much from the carbon paper, yet," he said. "It can be done, but it's slow going." He handed her the sheet of writing paper where he had copied what he'd been able to figure out so far.

She sat at the table and read out loud. " 'CU: Sit down, gentlemen. Would anyone care for a drink?

" 'HL: We don't have time for that. Let's get on with it. I asked all of you to come into town tonight because I figured all of us whose places abut the North Platte have been talking about our problem long enough. It's time we do something about it. I took a chance—' "

"That's as far as I got," Billy said. He picked up the carbon paper from which he had been reading and held it against the window. "Look, if you hold it up to the light, you can make out the words pretty good. Some of the letters are more distinct than others." He frowned. "Some of them you can't make out at all. It seems like, though, you can usually figure out what's supposed to be there if you're able to read the rest of the word. It's kind of like working one of those word puzzles."

"Could I see it?" Jill asked. Billy handed her the paper, and she, too, held it to the light. "I see what you mean."

"Also," Billy added, "you can flip the paper to the carbonized side. The individual letters are clearer and a whole lot easier to recognize on that side."

She turned the paper over. Where the typewriter's typing bars struck, the carbon was deposited on the second sheet of white paper to make the copy, and every time the bar hit, it left a distinct impression of the typing bar's letter on the carbon. "I see what you mean," Jill said, "it is clearer. Why aren't you try-ing to read it from this side?"

"Well, the problem is everything on that side shows up backward. It's like a foreign language. It would take me forever to figure it out."

Jill studied the paper for a bit, and her eyebrows rose. She tossed Billy a look that for the briefest second he thought might be suggesting he was none too bright.

"Come here, Billy," she said. She led him across the room to the chiffonier. Hanging on the wall above the chest of drawers was a looking glass. She held the carbonized side of the paper in front of it, turned to Billy, and smiled.

Billy looked at both of their images in the mirror. Jill's eyes were locked on him, and he dropped his gaze to the image of the typing on the back side of the carbon paper Jill held up. As soon as he did, he let out an embarrassed chuckle, scratched the back of his head, and said, "Well, I'll be switched."

Jill stood before the mirror slowly reading while Billy penciled what she read.

HL: I took a chance and told Cal here what I'm thinking right from the beginning. And I'll let all of you know right now that Cal is against what I'm proposing we do. He says it's illegal as hell, but I told him, and I'll tell all of you, if a man protecting what's rightfully his is illegal, call me an outlaw because I will do it every time.

I like Cal, but Cal is a lawyer, and the way I figure it, it's the lawyers that have got us into this mess in the first place. When it was just the cattlemen ruling the roost down at the legislature in Cheyenne, we didn't have these problems. But now that we've got us a bunch of lawyers down there, too, problems like this are always cropping up.

PM: Whatever you've got in mind, let's hear it, because I am up for anything. I am, by God, finished with giving up my water to these farmers. And the final insult as far as I'm concerned is the lawmakers saying it's fine for them to come in and condemn my land. Condemn my land, God-damn it.

CU: Phil, I believe you're misconstruing what is meant by the use of the word "condemn" in this sense.

PM: I ain't misconstruing a damned thing, lawyer. I know what it means. It means some son of a bitch can come onto my place and cut a ditch from one end of it to the other. It means he can use my wheel to lift my water out of the river, run it into that ditch he's already scarred up my property with, and let it flow across my place over to his.

AP: Christ, Phil, I stay mad about this all the time. I can hardly eat or sleep because of it, but when I hear the way you put it, it makes me even madder than I was before.

FC: It's a hell of a note. That's all I can say. One hell of a Goddamned note.

CU: As I've explained to you before, it's not just a mat-ter of these farmers crossing your places with the water. They have to pay you for any damages to your land. If they lift the water from the river with your equipment, they're required to provide you reimbursement. The law looks out for your interests.

PM: Looks out for our interests, my ass. Whatever amount these farmers would pay me to do it, I'd pay them that much to stay away. Hell, I'd pay them that much and half-again more.

HL: I know you feel that way, Phil. And I know the rest of you feel the same.

FC: So what are you getting at, Henry? Why did you call

us down here to Cal's office in the middle of the night?

HL: I've taken it upon myself to visit with a couple of the county commissioners about our situation. As luck would have it, they are sympathetic.

AP: They can be sympathetic 'til pigs shit gold and it ain't going to change the law.

HL: You're right, Artie, it ain't, but maybe we can make the law work for us.

FC: How do you mean?

HL: Whenever somebody wants to condemn our land for an irrigation ditch, there has to be an appraisal made to determine how much the damage will be, and based on that damage, the appraisers decide how much the fellow doing the condemning is going to have to pay the landowner he's crossing.

AP: So?

HL: So, how would you like it if we were the ones who chose the appraisers?

AP: I reckon that would be fine, but I don't plan on running for county commissioner, and it's the commissioners who appoint the three appraisers. And, by the way, the last time I counted there were also three commissioners. You say you've only been talking to two.

HL: That's true, but it's the majority of the commissioners who decide which appraisers are appointed. We only need two commissioners who're willing to consider our . . . well, our suggestions.

FC: I expect all of this good will from the county commissioners ain't free. How much is it going to cost us for them to consider our suggestions, as you call it?

HL: I figure if we each toss five thousand into the pot, it

will be more than enough to take care of the commissioners, two of the three appraisers they appoint, and a fellow from down Amarillo way I've hired to kind of oversee things. There'll be his fee and some smaller amount for a couple of ruffians who already work for me who'll be helping him out.

PM: This is all fine, Henry, but what good is it?

HL: What do you mean, what good is it?

PM: So we stick a couple of hand-picked appraisers in the mix and make a few dollars more when they condemn our property than we would have before—so what? They're still condemning our land. There ain't no amount of money I'd be willing to take to have these bastards dig ditches across my property. No amount in the world.

HL: You won't have to, Phil. That's the beauty of it. The price will be set so high these farmers and sheep herders and small-time cattle breeders will never be able to come up with the funds. What will happen is they won't be able to raise the cash to pay for the condemnation, so they won't get the water. And everybody knows with a water right, you either use it or you lose it. If they don't get the water, obviously they can't use it, and they lose their right to have it. When that happens, they're out of business. Oh, sure, some of them will try to dig a few wells on their places, I suppose. They already have. But they can't get enough water that way to run much of an operation. They need flowing water, and for that they have to come to us. If we make it too expensive for them, what are they going to do? Eventually they'll go broke, the bankers will call in their loans, and they'll be through.

AP: I think you're right, Henry. They'll be through, and

I expect we might even be able to pick up their places for pennies on the dollar.

HL: That's right. In the end, giving you a handsome return on your five-thousand-dollar investment.

PM: That does sound good.

FC: Not so fast, boys. The way I understand this damned law, if these sodbusters don't like the numbers the appraisers come up with, they can appeal it to the district court. Ain't that right, Cal?

CU: It is, but something tells me Henry has already thought of that.

HL: You're right, Caldwell, I have. We all know Judge Fisher has certain problems.

PM: He's a damned drunk is what he is.

HL: You do have a way about you, don't you, Phil?

PM: I don't lie. I never have. I never will.

HL: The judge does have a fondness for the bottle, but I'm not talking just about that. Sure, it may be that fondness that'll make him ready to listen to what we have to propose in the first place, but what's going to make him see it our way is not his love for liquor, but his love for Sadie.

AP: Sadie, his wife? What's she got to do with any of this?

HL: She's suffering from tuberculosis, and it's getting worse. The judge wants to send her to a sanatorium down in Colorado, but it's expensive, and he doesn't have the money.

AP: Damn, Henry, you have thought it out, haven't you?

HL: I'm just trying to protect what we've worked so hard to build. It's no different than when we used to have to fight the damned Indians. It's just not as straightforward. Things are more complicated now and have to be handled in a different way. That's all. Personally, I'd just as soon shoot the sons of bitches. And I mean that, too. The way I figure it, we are fighting for our families here, and the battle lines are drawn. We are fighting for our way of life, and there's nothing in this world more sacred than that. If it comes down to it, I'd die to protect it, and I'd sure as hell kill to protect it. It's my hope, though, by doing things this way, we might avoid bloodshed.

FC: You're a good man, Henry, and you're right.

PM: That's for sure. And I'll have the five thousand to you first thing in the morning, soon as the bank opens up.

AP: Count me in.

FC: Same here.

CU: Now, I want to tell you fellows something. There are two reasons I wanted to be here tonight at your meeting. One is to make sure you each realize that bribing a public official is a felony punishable by up to five years in prison. Now, if I'm hearing right, you're talking about bribing two commissioners, two appraisers, and a district court judge. That's five separate crimes, so you'd be looking at up to twenty-five years a piece.

The next thing I want you to understand is I am disavowing myself of any participation in this. I want that clear. I want that understood. I am having nothing to do with it.

AP: By God, Caldwell, you're using your lawyering voice. You sound just like you do in the courtroom when you're saying things on the record.

CU: I wouldn't put it—uh, well, be that as it may. I

want it understood as the attorney for each one of you, it is my advice that you forget this conspiracy. Stop it now before it goes any further. As it stands right now, you have committed no crime. Merely talking about bribing an official is not illegal, but if you do some act to further these briberies—for instance, going to your banker for the funds, even if you never offer those funds to the official, you have committed a crime, and I want it known I am not a party to it.

HL: All right, Cal. You've made your point, but we are going ahead with it because it's the only thing left to do.

CU: Very well. Now that I've said my piece, I'll leave.

HL: That's fine. We'll lock up when we're finished. By the way, Cal, before you go, I want you to get something clear, too. You are our attorney, and everything we have discussed tonight was said in confidence.

CU: I understand, although in a situation like this I'm not sure the attorney–client privilege applies.

PM: If you know what's good for you, lawyer, it had better apply.

HL: Phil's right, Caldwell, it had better apply.

Jill placed the last piece of carbon paper with the others atop the chiffonier. "It stops there, Billy."

Billy put his pencil down and rubbed the cramp out of his right hand. "Well, there we have it. At least we will as soon as we figure out who all of these initials belong to. Walter Cosgrove was going to note at the end of the transcript who was present, but I reckon he got interrupted before he could. It shouldn't be hard to figure out who these fellas are, though, and when we do, we'll know who's behind the things that've been happening around here the last few days." He looked out the window at the traffic passing on Fourth Street.

"How do you mean?"

"I don't know how, but these fellas found out Unger had Simms make a record of their meeting in his office that night, and they killed him for it. They made it look like an accident, but they killed him just the same. And they were also after Bernard Simms."

"How do you suppose they found out Simms was writing it down?" Jill asked. She sat at the table beside Billy and rested her hands in her lap. She smelled of lilac perfume and furniture polish.

"I don't know how, but they did, and they killed Simms, too."

Two tiny lines furrowed into the space between her eyebrows. "But he was killed during the train robbery."

"That's right, but I think the robbery was a cover. They made Unger's murder look like an accident, and they made Simms's murder look like just another killing during the robbery, no more significant than the others who were killed."

"You mean you think those men murdered everyone on the train—or tried to—just to cover up the fact they wanted to kill Bernard Simms?"

Billy nodded. "That's what I think."

"My God, Billy, what kind of men are these?"

"The kind who're willing to do whatever it takes to get what they want."

"We have the transcript," Jill said. "Maybe we should take it to the sheriff. He could arrest them, and this would all be over."

Billy knew a lot of reasons he'd not be doing that. "No," he said.

"Why not?"

"First of all, I think the sheriff is in on it with them."

"No, that's silly. I mean, he's so nice. He even helped me find my job with Mrs. Jordan."

"That may be, Jill, but I expect he's the one who tipped them off that I had located Simms's shorthand notes and was having the reporter in Casper make a transcript. Besides you and Mrs. Simms, he's the only one who knew."

"Oh, Billy, I can't believe he'd do it. After all, he's the *sheriff.*"

"Yes, he is," Billy agreed, lifting the transcript and thumbing its pages. "But it's getting easier and easier to believe that supposedly good, upstanding citizens are capable of anything."

Jill glanced at the papers Billy held and nodded.

"My friend Hugo's chasing a Baptist deacon who slit an Indian agent's throat."

Billy dropped the papers back onto the tabletop and stood. It was hard for him to think sitting down. He needed to be on his feet. He needed to hear his boot heels hitting the floor. He shoved his hands into the front pockets of his jeans and began to pace back and forth across the room.

Only yesterday the situation had been a lot less complicated. Then Billy had thought he was dealing with only three men, the men who had robbed the train. Now it was clear that was not the case. Not only would he be facing Zeke Blood, but by the looks of Walter Cosgrove's office, he would be facing at least three other newly hired ruffians as well. But that was not the worst of it. Giving Blood and his men their orders were four of the largest landowners in the county. Was he really ready to go up against men like that?

Billy was turning this thought around, holding it up to the light, when Mrs. Jordan popped her head into his open doorway. "Jill, honey," she said, "we're about to start getting supper together. Would you set the table, please?"

Jill came to her feet. "Yes, ma'am, of course. I'll be right there."

The older woman gave them both a smile and started to leave. "Excuse me, Mrs. Jordan," Billy called out. "Before you go, I wonder if you might help me with something."

"Surely, if I can." The woman stepped into the room.

"You've lived in this area awhile, I suspect."

"Most of my life, yes."

"If I were to give you the initials of some men who own large parcels of land along the North Platte, do you think you could tell me their names?"

"I'm sure I could."

Billy crossed to the table and ran an index finger down the transcript. "The first one's initials are HL."

Without hesitation, Mrs. Jordan said, "That'd have to be Henry Lovett."

"Lovett, yes," Billy said. "He has a place just upriver from here, doesn't he?"

"That's right."

"Okay," Billy glanced down at the transcript, "how about PM, another fella with some land along the river."

"Phil McCutcheon. How many more have you got?" Mrs. Jordan asked, "Two?"

"Yes, ma'am, two."

"Then it'd probably be Artie Price and Fred Cooke."

"Yes, it must be. The other two sets of initials are AP and FC. How did you know?"

"Because those four, along with Cal Unger, are always in on something together. They figure they run everything from Pumpkin Buttes in the north to Laramie Peak in the south, and from the La Prele all the way east to the state line." She gave her strong jaw a quick tilt. "The sad truth," she added, "is in one way or another they probably do run it all." She motioned toward what Billy held. "What is it you have there, anyway?" she asked.

She held her hand out for the transcript, but Billy didn't offer it.

"I don't know, ma'am," he said, pulling the papers closer. "I think people have been killed because of these papers. Maybe

129

it's best if you not get involved." He looked toward Jill. "If I'd known what I had, I wouldn't've let Jill see it either."

The girl tossed him a frown. "If you hadn't," she said, "you'd still be trying to figure out what it said."

Billy smiled despite himself. "I reckon that's true."

"Now you've really whetted my curiosity," said Mrs. Jordan. "At least tell me who you think it is who's been killed because of those papers."

"Caldwell Unger and Bernard Simms. Also, indirectly, you might say, those men who lost their lives at the train robbery between here and Casper a few days ago."

"Oh, my word," said the woman. "But I thought Cal was killed in a hunting accident."

"I think it was made to appear that way, ma'am, but I don't think that's the way it happened."

"And you believe Henry Lovett and the others are involved?"

Billy hesitated. He might have already said too much, but he answered the woman's question anyway. "I do."

Mrs. Jordan moved to one of the chairs beside the table and sat down. She touched the fingers of her right hand to her lips. Billy watched as her eyes began to fill. "I feel for their wives," she said. "All their wives. It is a hard thing to lose a husband." She brushed away a tear that traced along her cheek. "Mirabel Simms and Grace Unger are two of my best friends. It must be even worse for them knowing their husbands were murdered."

"I don't believe they realize just what's happened, ma'am, and I think it's better for the time being if they don't know. Although Mrs. Simms has certain suspicions, I know she's not aware of it. She thinks, as everyone does, her husband was just one of the victims in the robbery. I'm not sure what all Mrs. Unger knows. I was unable to visit with her before she left for Nebraska."

Mrs. Jordan's head came up. "I beg your pardon?"

"I say, I wanted to speak with Mrs. Unger, but by the time I got to town, she'd already left for her sister's house in Nebraska."

The woman shook her index finger at the ceiling. "No, Mr. Young. You must be mistaken. Grace doesn't have a sister. At least not one I've ever heard about."

"She doesn't?"

"No, and she's not in Nebraska." Mrs. Jordan's lips pursed and her eyes narrowed. "I shouldn't say this, I don't suppose. She asked me to keep it to myself." She looked up at Billy and stared into him. After a bit she continued, "But something makes me think Grace would approve of my telling you." She gave her eyes one last wipe and pushed herself up from the chair. She seemed older now than she had a few minutes before, as though the talk of dying husbands had caused her to age. "Grace is staying in the little summer house she and Cal built up in the Laramie Mountains. It's about eight or ten miles from here toward the mining town of Esterbrook. I visited her and Cal there a couple of years ago right after they built the place. It's a little more rustic than their house here in town, although not by much. It's really nice, and it's in a lovely spot, very remote. A good place to be alone to grieve and to think. How did you get the idea she had gone to Nebraska?"

"From the sheriff."

"I cannot imagine where he would've come by such a notion, but I assure you, it's not true." She turned to Jill and said, "Well, young lady, I expect we'd best get busy if we're going to feed our hungry guests." She led Jill toward the door but stopped halfway there and faced Billy once again. "Is there any chance you might be wrong about all this?" she asked.

"No, ma'am. I wish I was, but I don't think so."

"Then if you wish to speak to Grace Unger, try her house on the mountain. I'm certain she's there. We spoke right after Cal's funeral, and she said she needed to get away."

CHAPTER THIRTEEN

Billy left town the next morning better than an hour before sunup while the streets were still deserted. He expected after Sheriff Linford had spread the word about his snooping around, Zeke Blood was looking for him as hard as Billy was looking for Blood, and unless Billy wanted to be bushwhacked from an open window, it wouldn't hurt to keep out of sight as much as possible. He had even decided to give up his room at the boarding house and make camp outside of town. That way he would not be putting Mrs. Jordan and Jill in needless danger.

Jill had told him of an out-of-the-way spot good for camping north of town along Antelope Creek. When he returned, that was where he'd stay. And perhaps Jill, once the supper dishes were washed, could join him at his camp and they'd share a cup of coffee under the stars.

He enjoyed being around Jill. He found his thoughts lingering on her more and more, but it was best if he no longer stayed at the boarding house. He didn't want to bring down on either her or her employer what he'd brought onto Walter Cosgrove.

After being cooped up in the stable, Badger was especially frisky that morning, and it was reassuring to Billy to feel the young horse's strength beneath him. Billy liked a spirited animal.

It was a pleasant ride. Despite the steady climb from the river town of Probity up to the Unger house, Billy made good time. There was a trail of sorts, at least in most places, and Billy enjoyed the exercise in the cool morning air.

When Mrs. Jordan had given him directions, she explained that because of the way the house was situated against a cliff in a stand of aspen, it was impossible to see until you were right upon it. She had said about a mile and a half after the trail petered out, Billy would come to a large boulder shaped like a buffalo. "It's impossible to miss," she had said, which made Billy a little uneasy. He'd been known to miss plenty of places people had told him were impossible to miss. Once he found the boulder he was to look toward the north. Only then would he be able to see the Unger house tucked deep into the trees.

That sounded like not only a good place to grieve and think, Billy told himself as Badger trotted along, but maybe a good place to hide.

As Billy made that observation, Badger brought him over a rise, and there he saw it. The rock was big as a barn, and sure enough, it had the unmistakable appearance of an enormous humped buffalo. Billy gave the gray's neck a pat. "Well, I'll be damned, Badger," he said. "Mrs. Jordan was right. Even I couldn't miss a rock like that."

He gigged the horse with his right spur, and as he did, the ground beside him exploded. A half second later there was the crack of rifle fire. Billy dove from the saddle, pulling his Marlin from the scabbard as he did. He hit the ground, rolled behind a stand of boulders, and grabbed a handful of gravel. He threw the gravel at Badger and shouted, "Heee-yah, horse, get outta here," and Badger loped off into the trees.

Billy had not seen where the shot came from, and because of all the granite in the area, there were enough echoes he was unable to tell by the sound. He took off his hat, and for a better view, he raised his head above the line of his cover. He scanned the rough terrain, looking for the gun smoke from the first shot and watching for the muzzle flash from the next, but he saw nothing, and no second shot came.

He levered a round into the Marlin and rested the octagonal barrel across the rock that protected him.

The shot might have come from any one of a thousand places. The best cover was not far away—less than a hundred yards—and any man with any marksmanship at all should have been able to shoot him out of the saddle with ease. Billy doubted it was Blood out there. If it had been, Billy would now be staring up into the morning sky, except his eyes would not be watching the scud of summertime clouds. Maybe, he told himself, the shot had been nothing more than a warning.

"You out there, shooter," he called, "unless your name happens to be Zeke Blood, I mean you no harm." Billy figured being honest would do no damage. If in the unlikely event it did turn out to be Blood, the man already knew Billy's intentions. "If you are Mr. Blood, let's put away our rifles and settle our differences up close, face-to-face."

Billy had a long wait with no response. Finally, a voice called out, "What's your name, mister?" And to Billy's surprise, it was the voice of a woman.

"My name's Billy Young. I got a place west of here up by Casper just below the mountain."

"What causes you to leave your mountain and come all the way over here to this one?"

"I'm searching for a woman by the name of Grace Unger. Are you by any chance her?"

"What do you want her for?"

"I want to talk to her about her husband."

There was another long pause. Then the voice asked, "What about him?"

"I would like to discuss his death." Billy started to say more but stopped himself.

"Go on. Keep talking."

"The things I have to say, I'll say only to Mrs. Unger. And, even if you are Mrs. Unger, I'll not say them to you in a shout."

There was another one of those pauses. "Fetch your horse, Mr. Young, and ride forward. When you do, put your rifle back in its scabbard, hold your reins high with your left hand, and keep your right hand in the air where I can see it."

Billy stuck his hat back on his head, took in a deep breath, and stepped from behind his cover. He assumed he was not about to get shot, but it was still a troublesome feeling walking from the rocks where he was hiding across the open space to the stand of trees where Badger had run. When he got to his horse, he gasped and let out the breath he'd not realized he'd been holding.

"Well, Badge," Billy said as he climbed aboard the gray, "I figure this woman'll do one of two things. Either shoot me dead or give me a cup of coffee. If she does the latter, I promise you I will fill your bag with oats." He shoved the Marlin into the scabbard and took the reins with his left hand. He wheeled the horse around, aimed him at the buffalo rock, and gave him some spur. "If she does the former, you're on your own."

Billy approached the rock at a walk, his right hand in the air.

"That's far enough," the voice said, and a woman in her late forties stood from behind a three-foot-high rock to Billy's left.

She held a large-frame Colt slide-action long gun. Billy realized from the raised peep sight and the confident manner in which she cradled the weapon that if she'd wanted him dead, that's what he would be.

When she noticed Billy staring at the gun, she said, "A woman out here can't be too careful."

"No, ma'am, I reckon not."

"Now let your reins dangle and place both hands on your saddle horn where I can see them."

She wore a man's heavy twilled pants, a chambray shirt, and a narrow-brimmed hat. She had refined good looks, which seemed out of place in the rough garb, but she wore the clothes well, as though she was accustomed to such attire.

Billy did as he was told and placed his hands, one atop the other, on his saddle horn. "Are you Mrs. Unger?" he asked.

"I am. Now, what do you have to say?"

Billy nodded toward the rifle the woman held. "Was that Colt Lightning your husband's?" Billy asked.

"It was." She raised it higher. "Although I enjoy shooting more than he did."

"I believe you, ma'am. It's just seeing such a fine weapon makes me more convinced than ever of what I came here to talk to you about."

"Get on with it, mister."

"I was thinking it doesn't make sense a man would go hunting with an old out-of-date Spencer when he has a piece like that slide-action available."

Grace Unger's eyes widened. "What is it you want, young man?"

Billy smiled. "Well, I was sorta hoping for a cup of morning coffee, if it wouldn't be too much trouble."

Badger gave a pleased snort and blew oat dust through the air holes of his feed bag.

"Enjoy your breakfast, there, Badge. I'll be back in a while." He gave the animal a pat on the shoulder and stepped up onto the porch of the Ungers' summer house.

The place was a small, two-story white frame with green shutters and shingles. It had gingerbread trim and spindled porch rails that were also painted green. Although the fashionable style of the place seemed odd out here in the middle of nowhere, the house's green-and-white color scheme brought it together in a pleasing way with the surrounding stand of aspen.

Mrs. Unger had gone in ahead of him while he tended to his

horse, and Billy knocked on the screened front door.

"Let yourself in," the woman called from the rear of the house. "I'm in the kitchen."

Billy stepped in and followed the woman's voice as she said, "There was coffee already made, but I just put on a fresh pot. It should be ready in a bit."

The kitchen was large, much larger than the parlor through which Billy had just passed. A coffee pot set atop a modern, black-and-chrome Findlay cook stove, and in the corner was a heavy oak eating table surrounded by four matching chairs. In the center of the table was a plate of biscuits. Next to the biscuits was a Mason jar of what looked to be blackberry preserves.

"Have a seat, Mr. Young, and help yourself to a biscuit."

"Thank you, ma'am, I will." Billy was starved. He'd left Mrs. Jordan's before breakfast, and these biscuits looked to be just the thing.

"I'm sorry they're not hot," Mrs. Unger apologized. "I made them last night."

"They look delicious, ma'am," Billy said as he spread on a helping of preserves.

The woman allowed him to swallow a couple of bites before she asked, "How did you find me?"

Billy hoped his answer would not cause a rift between friends. "Mrs. Jordan," he said. "She mentioned you didn't want anyone to know where you'd gone, but she said she doubted you would mind."

"Libby Jordan's no fool. If she felt it was important we meet, I expect I need to hear whatever it is you have to say."

Billy set the last bite of his biscuit onto the table in front of him. "I'll be blunt, Mrs. Unger. It is my belief your husband was not killed by accident. Based on some things told to me by Sheriff Linford, I believe you suspect the same."

"I do, and I think that although our sheriff is a very small frog in this pond, he knows more about it all than he lets on. Unfortunately, I came to that conclusion after I had already voiced to him my doubt that Cal would go hunting at all, much less under the circumstances he supposedly did."

Billy nodded. "I suspect the sheriff of certain things myself."

"The man is not trustworthy," said the woman. "He will always be loyal to those he feels are in power, whoever they might be. That sort of man should never be told too much, and letting him know how I felt about the accident was foolish."

"How familiar were you with your husband's business affairs?"

"I'm certain there were many things in my husband's practice I was not aware of, although, if he found some situation troubling, he often discussed it with me. I know he valued my opinion."

"Are you aware of a meeting he had the night before his death with a group of ranchers who own property along the river?"

The woman's lips thinned, and she stood and walked to the stove. "The coffee's ready," she said. She took two cups from a cupboard and filled them. "Would you care for sugar? I'm afraid I haven't any cream."

Billy pointed out to the woman that he'd never turned down the offer of sugar in his life.

She placed two spoonfuls into his coffee but left hers unsweetened. She brought the two cups to the table, set Billy's beside what was left of his biscuit, and sat down. "Yes, Mr. Young," she answered, "I know of the meeting you're referring to."

"I can't prove it, but I believe it is the men your husband had the meeting with who are responsible for his death. I also believe these same men ordered the robbery of a train and the murder of several people on that train in an effort to cover up killing Bernard Simms."

Billy took a sip of the coffee and told Grace Unger all he knew. She listened to his story in silence, and when he finished she said, "I feared Henry and the others were behind Cal's death."

"Tell me about the meeting your husband had and of the last hours before he died."

"Cal told me some of what Henry Lovett planned. I knew, for instance, it was Henry's intention to arrange it so he could select the appraisers who were to determine the cost of ditches and the damage to the land. There was never anything mentioned specifically about bribery, so, frankly, I didn't think much about it. Henry and his friends, including my husband, have been manipulating things around here in one way or another for more than twenty years. To the best of my knowledge, though, it was never through bribery or other illegal means. Cal did seem nervous that night before he left for his office, which was unlike him. My husband was always very much in control, Mr. Young, but that night he seemed unsettled."

"Did he tell you he'd arranged for Bernard Simms to make a record of the meeting?"

"No, he didn't, but I learned of that the next morning when Henry, Phil McCutcheon, and the other man came to our house."

"What other man?"

"I didn't know him. He was young, but not as young as you. He was in his late twenties, I suppose, maybe early thirties."

"Did he wear a black leather vest, by chance, and was he armed?"

"I believe his vest was leather, and, yes, I'm certain he was armed." She shrugged, "But, of course, that's hardly unusual."

"No," Billy acknowledged, "but did he wear his gun the way

a gunfighter might?"

"I'm not certain I would know how a gunfighter might wear his gun, but I am certain of one thing. This man was no cowboy."

Billy sipped his coffee. "No," he agreed, "that man is no cowboy. His name is Zeke Blood."

"Isn't that the name you called out when you were behind the rocks?"

"Yes, ma'am, it is. He murdered my brother and several others, and unless he gets me first, I plan to kill him."

"He might be a hard one to kill. He had a mean look about him. I even described him that way to my husband. I answered the door that morning, and when I told Cal who was there, I said, 'It's Henry and Phil, and a mean-looking stranger is with them.' Who is he, Mr. Young? Do you know?"

"He's the killer Lovett brought up from Texas. Why did they come to your house that morning?"

"They came to confront my husband."

"Confront him?"

"That's right. Cal took them into the parlor, but Cal's own uneasiness made me uncomfortable, and I admit to eavesdropping on their conversation." She stiffened in her chair a bit. "That is not a thing I do, Mr. Young, eavesdrop. That's not my way."

"No, ma'am. I'm sure it's not."

"But I was concerned. Cal took them into the parlor, and the first thing said was Henry asked Cal who the man was. At first Cal seemed confused, as though he had no idea what Henry was talking about. But then Henry lost his temper. I had never heard Henry, or anyone else, for that matter, speak to Caldwell Unger in the manner Henry spoke that morning. He shouted profanity, screaming that Cal knew what man he was talking about. Henry indicated the third man who was with them, this Mr. Blood, had been waiting outside the office the night before, and when Cal left through the front door, Mr. Blood had seen another man leave the office by the side door. Cal and this other man met in the street before they went their separate ways."

"That would have been Bernard Simms," Billy said.

"Yes, and finally Cal admitted to Henry that it was Bernard. Cal told Henry that because of what Henry was planning to do regarding the ditch appraisals, that he, Cal, wanted proof that he had no part in what was taking place. Cal pointed out that he had represented Henry and the others for years, and because they had all been involved in many activities together, it would be assumed by everyone, should it come to light what was going on, that Cal was a part of this scheme as well. Cal told Henry he would not allow that to happen. He assured Henry he had no intention of ever bringing Bernard's transcript to light unless things did eventually go sour and Cal was accused of some wrongdoing by the authorities. Otherwise, it would never see the light of day, but Cal intended to keep it for that reason just in case."

"How did Henry Lovett and Phil McCutcheon react to that?" Billy asked.

"They were still not pleased, but my husband was a very persuasive man, Mr. Young, and it seemed, to me at least, that they accepted that he meant them no harm. He was merely trying to protect himself should things go badly. They threatened if he ever did use it against them, or if Bernard Simms ever did, both he and Simms would regret it, but they left without incident, and it seemed to be over."

"Did you speak to your husband after they left?"

"Yes, I told him I'd heard everything."

"What was his reaction to Lovett and the others' discovering he'd had the stenographer writing down what they said?"

"I loved my husband very much, Mr. Young. We had been

married for almost thirty years. I knew him well. He tried to pretend it meant nothing, but he was concerned. I could see it in his eyes. I could hear the worry between his words. It was only a little after six in the morning, and he didn't, as a rule, leave for work so early, but that morning he said he wanted to let Bernard know that Lovett and the others knew what he and Bernard had done. Cal said he was going to stop by Simms's house, and from there he would go to work." She paused and cleared her throat. "When he left that morning, it was the last time I saw him."

She stood, crossed to the stove, and came back with the coffee pot. She refilled both of their cups and took the pot to the sink where she pumped water into it and rinsed out the grounds. Billy sipped his coffee and waited.

After a bit she returned to the table and sat. In a composed, even voice she said, "At first it was my intention to tell the sheriff what had happened. As you know, I even mentioned how unlikely I felt it was that Cal, who had no love for the activity, would go hunting in the middle of the day with a gun he'd not fired in decades. But I realized as I was speaking to the sheriff that if my suspicion that it was no accident was true, it was not wise to let anyone know I was aware of what had happened the night before."

"But, even though you didn't mention it, you still didn't feel safe in town."

"No, I led the sheriff to believe I was going to Nebraska, but I came here as soon as the funeral was over. Henry Lovett is aware Cal often spoke to me regarding his practice, and my knowing Henry was aware of that made me feel uneasy. That's why I came up here, or at least it was one of the reasons." She looked about the kitchen. "I love this house Cal and I built. It makes me feel closer to him to be here. I told myself that was the main reason I came. Despite Henry's anger that morning and the suspicious nature of Cal's death, I couldn't allow myself to believe Henry would ever harm Cal or me. I've known Henry Lovett even longer than I knew Cal." She rested her forearms on the table and seemed very tired. "Now, though, after hearing the things you know and putting them together with what I know, I expect my hopes for Henry were misplaced."

Billy picked up his last bite of biscuit and started to eat it but stopped himself. "I guess that's the real reason I rode out to see you, Mrs. Unger. I know it was Zeke Blood who killed my brother, and I know now I could probably find him out at the Lovett place. But I also realize Blood is an accomplished gunman, and when we meet, things may not turn out as I'd like. I'm embarrassed to admit it, but I fear the worst may happen, and there are some things I'd like to understand before it does."

"What's that, young man?"

"I guess I'd like to understand what kind of men these people are. Oh, I understand Blood well enough. He's nothing more than a cold-blooded killer, but it's these others I can't figure out."

Mrs. Unger lifted her cup. She held it with both hands, but she didn't raise it to drink. "Two weeks ago I might've told you they were good, hard-working family men. I might've told you they were brave men who built this land, who fought Indians and rustlers, who faced subzero winters and scorching summers. I might've told you they were the kind of ingenious men who could create a thriving agricultural industry in a place with topsoil no deeper than the end of my thumb and doesn't get enough water during the course of a year to fill a hat. Two weeks ago I might've told you they were friends of mine and my husband's." She sipped from her cup, lowered it to the table, and lifted her eyes to Billy. "But that was two weeks ago. I know them better now. Now I know out of greed or pride or both, they are men capable of ordering the deaths of both friends and strangers."

"Then how do we ever know what someone's like?" Billy asked. "You describe these people, and they sound the same as men I've known all my life. They sound like my own neighbors. Heck, ma'am, they even sound like my father or my brother. They could be my own blood."

Mrs. Unger nodded.

Billy paused, took in a deep breath, and looked across at the older woman, "Can you help me to understand?" he asked. "If men like these are capable of doing these things, how are we ever supposed to tell the good from the bad?"

"I expect if you could measure it," Mrs. Unger pointed out, "I doubt you'd find many folks who are heavily weighted with either good or bad. I expect, if you looked at it hard enough, what you'd discover is most folks carry around a whole lot of both."

CHAPTER FOURTEEN

The next day was a Sunday, and early that morning, while Mrs. Unger packed, Billy hitched her brown mare to the Stanhope Phaeton parked in the small barn. He tied Badger's reins to the back, drove the carriage to the front of the house, and waited for the woman to come out.

A thunderstorm had struck the previous afternoon as Billy visited with Mrs. Unger, and rather than fight the rain, wind, and pea-sized hail that came along with it, Billy had spent the rest of the day and night at the Unger house, sleeping on a not-very-comfortable sofa in the parlor.

Billy was impressed with Grace Unger. She was a strong woman, sure of herself and confident in what needed to be done now that she felt she understood the situation.

During their conversation in the kitchen, Billy had fetched from his saddlebag the handwritten transcript of the meeting in Mr. Unger's office. The woman read it, and when she finished, she said, "There's only one choice we have."

"What's that?" Billy had asked. He was eager to hear her suggestion as to how to proceed. Billy himself had no better idea than riding to the Lovett place and calling Zeke Blood to task for his crimes—a poor plan that would no doubt get him killed

"This transcription of their meeting," Mrs. Unger said, "does not prove anyone's involvement in Cal's death, or your brother's, or any of the others, but it does show their conspiracy to bribe public officials."

"Yes, ma'am," Billy had agreed, "it does. But it only shows they were discussing it. According to what your husband told them right there in the transcript, if they didn't do something toward completing the bribery, they haven't really committed a crime. I doubt they ever went much further with the plan considering everything fell apart the day after they held that meeting."

"No," Mrs. Unger said, "I'm sure they didn't, not unless Henry Lovett is a bigger fool than I know him to be."

"Then what are you saying?" Whatever it was the woman had in mind was eluding Billy.

"Why did my husband die, Mr. Young?"

"Why?"

"Yes, sir. Why did he die and your brother and Bernard Simms as well? Why were they killed?"

"Because Lovett and the others didn't want what transpired at the meeting to become known."

"Exactly."

Billy was still not sure where the woman was going.

"They did not want the transcript discovered," Mrs. Unger went on. "That's also why they destroyed the court stenographer's office in Casper. They stole the original and the copy of the transcript from there, and now, except for me, Henry and the others feel their worries are over. They don't know for sure how much I know, but I suspect they are not too worried about it since they assume I'm now off somewhere in Nebraska. They have no way of knowing you figured out a way to obtain a copy of the transcript from the carbons."

Billy thought about that for a moment and said, "So now that they've killed the only two men at the meeting who could threaten their plans and they've obtained the only copies of the transcript that they believe exist, you're saying they can go ahead and approach the commissioners after all?"

"As far as they know, they can, and they may already have, but even if they have, the commissioners would deny it, so we'd still have no way to prove the bribery."

Billy was confused. "So what are you getting at? The transcript doesn't prove they killed anyone, and it doesn't prove they've bribed anyone. I'm sorry, Mrs. Unger, but I don't understand."

"I'm saying even though we may not be able to bring them to punishment, we can at least put a stop to all this. I'm convinced once they realize I'm not off in Nebraska, I, too, will soon be killed. They can't be sure I know anything, but they'll not be willing to risk it. Since Probity is the place I plan to spend the rest of my days—and I hope there will be a lot of days left to spend—I can't have Henry and his friends looking to kill me." There was an amused sparkle in her eye at that last observation.

"I can see how that might be a problem," Billy allowed.

The woman pointed an index finger at the ceiling and gave it a shake. "There is a way, however," she said, "that we can make them think twice before they harm me because even if they made my death appear to be an accident, they would still be suspected. At the same time we can prevent them from bribing the county commissioners and stealing the land from the farmers and small ranchers who want to take water from the North Platte River. We won't be doing anything that'd get them convicted in a court of law, unfortunately, but we could stop them in their tracks."

Billy was beginning to comprehend what she had in mind. There was only one way they could accomplish all of that.

He picked up his handwritten papers she'd placed on the table in front of them. "We can make this transcript public," he said.

And Mrs. Unger smiled.

★ ★ ★ ★ ★

She came out of the house carrying a goatskin valise, and Billy jumped from the phaeton and took it from her. She locked the door as Billy loaded the valise into the back of the carriage.

The eastern sky was just turning pink, and Billy checked his watch. If the going wasn't too slow from the previous day's rain, he expected they would be pulling into Probity at about mid-morning—perfect timing.

In addition to her valise, Mrs. Unger also came out of the house carrying a wicker basket covered with a towel. "I've prepared us some egg and sausage sandwiches," she said, "since we're setting off without our breakfast."

They had spent the evening chatting, and Billy told her about Frank and his parents and their place at Casper Mountain. She was an easy woman to talk to, and their conversation had been relaxed.

Sometime during the course of the evening, he had mentioned Jill Springer and how his mind kept leaping back to her no matter how hard he tried to point it in another direction.

"It could be you're falling in love, Mr. Young." She continued to refer to him as Mr. Young even though he'd told her to call him Billy.

Billy was shocked to think the woman might hold such a silly notion as his falling in love, and he denied that possibility. When he did, Mrs. Unger supplied him with another of her smiles.

"Get up there," Billy said, smacking the reins against the brown mare's rump, and the phaeton lurched from the yard of the Ungers' summer house.

The going was slow. Conditions were not as arid on the mountain as they were down below, but rain was not common up here either, and after the kind of storm that hit the day before, the ground, particularly in the low places, was soupy with mud.

Once they made it the mile and a half past the buffalo rock and got onto the trail, the going became easier, and Mrs. Unger opened her basket and handed Billy a sandwich.

The egg was fried just the way Billy liked—soft at the yolk and fringed with brown lace. It had been a while since he'd enjoyed a woman's cooking. Billy's mother had always cooked for the family. She'd also helped Orozco with meals for the hands. After she died, Billy had taken over both of those chores, and he was surprised to discover how much work was involved, especially in the summer when they hired on extra men.

"I hope this works," Billy said, holding the reins with one hand and his sandwich with the other. He didn't elaborate on what it was he hoped worked. He didn't have to.

"There's no reason why it shouldn't," said Mrs. Unger. She draped a napkin over her lap, broke her sandwich in quarters, picked up one of the quarters, and held it as she spoke. "Once the truth is out, Henry and the others won't do anything. They can't. I suspect they'll be making themselves very scarce around Probity for a while."

"What about bringing out the whole truth?" Billy asked.

"You mean about the killings as well as their bribery plot?"

"I do. The killings are the reason I'm here, Mrs. Unger."

"I wish we could, but it would be our word against theirs. I'm certain people would believe Lovett and his friends capable of bribery, especially when we have the transcript to back it up, but without proof, I don't think anyone is ready to accept the rest of it."

"Well, I'm glad what we're doing will help protect you, and I'm glad it'll ruin their future schemes, but it doesn't help me, Mrs. Unger."

"You mean as far as Blood?"

"That's right."

"I was looking for a way to talk to you about that, Mr. Young. I realize you're a very competent young man. That was clear to me yesterday when I fired the warning shot in your direction. You remained cool in what you could've only perceived as a dire situation. Already you have brought two of the killers from the train robbery to justice, and you have discovered the name and whereabouts of the third." She placed her hand on his forearm, and he turned to look at her. "Your brother would not ask any more from you, Billy. You are competent, but even as mean as they were, the two men you've dealt with so far were fools. I expect Zeke Blood is something different."

"I expect he is."

"So leave it alone, or at least wait until you have some help."

"What help? Sheriff Linford?" She offered him no response. "My brother was thinking of me at the moment he died, Mrs. Unger. Jeets Duvall had his pistol leveled at my face when Frank charged him and caused the shot to go wide. It was while Frank was protecting me that Zeke Blood killed him. It could be Blood does have the advantage. I expect he does, but that doesn't change what I have to do."

Billy wanted to tell her the rest of it, but he couldn't find the words, and so he finished his sandwich in silence.

A new thought had occurred to him in the last couple of days, and he wished he knew how to explain it to her. He didn't have it figured out exactly yet—and he wasn't sure he ever would—but he felt there had to be some balance in this world. He believed there *was* right and wrong. There *was* good and evil. Maybe she was correct. If you weighed most men out, they might have plenty of both. But it went beyond that. Men's deeds could create evil. That was proven to Billy by what happened at the train. And if evil could be created, so could good.

His skills compared to Zeke Blood's didn't matter. Ignoring the odds against the success of bringing justice to his brother's killer and going ahead anyway despite those odds, to Billy's way of thinking, was good. It by itself was a good thing. Success or failure in the doing of it didn't affect whether the deed itself was good, and maybe the doing of the deed could in some way balance out the evil that was done beside the tracks.

It didn't make a lot of sense. He wasn't sure this notion could withstand the glare of too much light, but Billy knew inside himself it was true. For his brother's sake, there had to be some kind of balance. He wished he had enough skill with words to explain it to Mrs. Unger.

Then there was the other. And this was a thought—a feeling, really—he could have explained to her, but he chose not to. He didn't even want to admit it to himself. He tried his best to fend the feeling off, but it refused to be beaten back.

Billy *wanted* to kill Zeke Blood. He wanted to kill him because of the pleasure he knew it would bring to see his brother's murderer lying in the sand with a hole in his chest—a hole created by the smoking revolver clutched in Billy's fist.

He kept that feeling to himself.

The closer they got to the prairie, the less it had rained, and now the trail was almost dry. Billy clucked and gave the reins a snap to speed the mare along.

"You won't be leaving it alone, will you, Mr. Young?"

Billy shook his head. "No, ma'am. I know you're right about everything you say, but, even so, before it's done, one way or the other, I'll be killing Blood or he'll be killing me.

CHAPTER FIFTEEN

When Billy and Mrs. Unger crossed the bridge into Probity, the streets were quiet. It was ten-thirty on Sunday morning, and none of the shops were open. There was some activity around the depot and the telegraph office, but even those usually hectic places showed few signs of life.

"The Community Church is straight up Center Street at the top of the hill," Mrs. Unger said. "Just about everyone in town will be there."

"Well," said Billy, "I guess that's what we want, right?"

"Yes, just what we want." When she said it, Billy thought he heard a twinge of nervousness, but on second thought he decided he might have only thought he'd heard it because he was filtering it through the screen of his own jumpy nerves.

They drove up the rise from the river to the east side of town, and Billy could see before they arrived that the place was crowded. Wagons, carriages, and saddle horses filled the area in front of the church, and Billy drove the phaeton around to the back and parked in the shade of a cottonwood tree.

As he pulled to a stop, Mrs. Unger turned in her seat and opened the valise. The transcript was on top, and she pulled it out. "Here we go," she said as she dropped out of the buggy.

There was a door in the back of the church, but Mrs. Unger said, "Let's go around front and make a grand entrance."

Billy looked at the tall, steepled white building and was uneasy. "I'm not sure about this, Mrs. Unger. Do you think we should do this in a church?"

"Why not? We want to get their attention, don't we?"

"It doesn't seem right. Like it might even bring bad luck."

Mrs. Unger stopped, and Billy stopped beside her. "Listen to me, Mr. Young. If these men can order the murder of innocent people during the week and righteously attend services on Sunday, there's nothing wrong with what we plan to do."

After giving that some thought, Billy nodded, and Mrs. Unger led the way to the front of the building. They climbed the four stone steps to the broad double doors and went inside. An usher met them. He smiled and started to speak, but Mrs. Unger pushed past him without a word.

The place was large and every pew was filled. The congregation was in the middle of a hymn, but the volume lessened as Mrs. Unger and Billy strode up the center aisle.

With all of those eyes on him, Billy became aware of the weight of the forty-five on his hip, and he felt embarrassed. He'd never carried a weapon into a church before and he could feel the heat of everyone's gaze.

In the front of the sanctuary was a raised section that held a pulpit. Behind the pulpit stood a befuddled-looking minister who watched as Mrs. Unger and Billy walked toward him. Behind the minister was a robed choir of a dozen or so, and they, too, shared the minister's confused expression. To the right of the pulpit was an upright piano being played by an elderly woman who was so intent on reading her sheet music she appeared not to notice them.

By the time Billy and Mrs. Unger reached the front of the sanctuary, the singing had trickled to a stop, and once the singing had stopped, the elderly piano player stopped playing as well.

Mrs. Unger nodded toward the pastor and turned and faced the assembly.

"Good morning, everyone," she said. She almost sounded cheery, but there was a darker tone beneath her words. "I'm sorry to interrupt the services this way, but there's something important I want all of you to hear, and I couldn't think of any other time when everyone was all together."

She nodded toward a broad-shouldered man in the front row. "I see you're here, Henry. And Phil. And Artie. Where's Frank?" She stood on her tiptoes. "Oh, yes," she said, pointing toward the back, "there he is."

Billy would not have recognized any of these men, and he guessed part of the reason she singled them out was so he would know who they were and where they were sitting. He scanned the crowd looking for a face he *would* recognize—Zeke Blood—but Blood was not there. Billy did spot Mrs. Jordan and Jill at the end of a pew in the right-hand section and gave them a quick nod of hello.

"What is it you're doing here, Grace?" Lovett asked. Billy could see worry, and maybe fear, in the man's washed-out blue eyes. He shoved a thumb toward Billy. "And this fella you brought in here with you, who is he that he'd wear a sidearm into the house of the Lord?"

"Now don't be getting all sanctimonious, Henry. You're not in a position to be casting stones."

She held up the transcript and said, "The night before my husband was killed—" She dropped her eyes to Henry when she said the word *killed*. "—there was a meeting held at Cal's office."

It seemed to dawn on Lovett what Mrs. Unger was up to. He rose to his feet. "What's this all about?" he asked, and before she could answer, he added, "Don't do it. I warn you."

"Shut up, Henry Lovett," Mrs. Unger snapped, and there was a gasp from the congregation. "You warn me, do you? What

are you warning me of, Henry? The possibility of a hunting accident?"

Lovett stiffened but didn't respond.

"There was a meeting the night before Cal was killed. At that
meeting were Henry, Artie, Phil, Frank, and my husband. There
was another man there, but only Cal knew he was present. It
was Bernard Simms." She directed another glare at Lovett.
"The late Bernard Simms," she added. She found Mrs. Simms
in the crowd and said, "I'm sorry, Mirabel, for your loss. There
seem to've been a number of new widows created around here
and in Casper, too, over the course of the last week."

Lovett was still standing. "Don't do this, Grace," he repeated.

Mrs. Unger ignored him. "Bernard listened in on the meeting and wrote in his shorthand everything that transpired." She
took a deep breath and raised the pages. "This is what was
discussed that night, word-for-word. All of you listen to what
these men had to say. It's important you know. It starts with my
husband speaking. 'Sit down, gentlemen,' " she began. " 'Would
anyone care for a drink?' "

As Mrs. Unger read, the room was silent. Even the children
seemed to realize something rare was taking place, and they sat
quietly, their hands folded in their laps. Midway through, Henry
Lovett dropped back into his seat. As Billy watched him,
Lovett's eyes seemed to die. They seemed to sink into his face.
His broad shoulders sagged.

Mrs. Unger read every word, and when she finished, she
folded the papers in half and lifted her gaze to the still-silent
crowd.

After a bit, a man stood in the back, and, in a voice it seemed
he had to force to work, he croaked out, "I want you to know,
Grace Unger—I want all of you to know—we on the county
commission were never offered any money by Henry Lovett or
anyone else to do anything like was spoke about in that thing

she just read. None of us was. I'd swear to it."

"Thank you for that, Michael," Mrs. Unger said. "I never expected you to say anything else." She turned to Lovett. "But it's out now, Henry." The man did not look up to meet her scrutiny, so she walked over to him and bent low so she could see into his eyes. She shook his shoulder to get his attention. "I say it's out now, Henry, so you can stop what you've done to keep it from getting out. It's finished, all of it, and you would do well to let it stay that way."

Lovett lifted a gaunt hand and pointed at the papers Grace Unger held. "Where—" he swallowed hard, pushing something away that was plugging his gullet. "—where did you get that?"

Mrs. Unger smiled. "You're surprised, aren't you, Henry? You thought you'd taken care of this little problem." She waggled the papers at him. "Well, sir, you didn't. You almost did, God knows, but you didn't get it done." She motioned toward Billy. "Billy Young here pieced it together from evidence your ruffians foolishly left behind in the court stenographer's office in Casper."

Lovett's eyebrows went up, and he looked across at Billy. He took Billy in and turned to a boy sitting beside him who was a couple of years younger than Billy and whispered in the boy's ear. The boy rose, made his way down the aisle, and left the church.

"What do you mean," Lovett asked, "he pieced it together?"

"Just what I said, Henry. Your henchmen took the original and the copy of the transcript the reporter in Casper produced from Bernard Simms's notes, but they left behind the carbon paper he used. Mr. Young was able to create this—" She shook the papers again, almost taunting him with them. "—by using those carbons."

Lovett shoved back a comma of white hair that had fallen across his forehead. "That's a pack of lies," he said, rising to his feet. He seemed to have found an energy that had not been there a moment before. "Everything you've read and everything you've said since you broke in here this morning and interrupted our worship service has been nothing but a pack of lies." He nodded toward Billy. "Something this fella made up." He stepped out of the pew and walked toward her. Billy tensed, ready to knock this reedy old man to the floor if he attempted anything with the woman. Instead of attacking her, though, Lovett extended his arms to embrace her, but Grace Unger would have none of it and pushed him away.

He shook his head and smiled with the patience of Job. "Grace," he said, "I know how hard Cal's death has been on you. It's been hard on us all." He turned and found Mrs. Simms among the gape-mouthed onlookers. "And Bernard's death coming so close to Cal's, it's been a nightmare. It has. It has been a nightmare for the entire community. But we'll get through this. We'll all get through this horrible time together." As he spoke that last, the door to the sanctuary opened and in walked the boy who left a few moments earlier. Behind him came Sheriff Linford.

Lovett turned and said, "Good, Sheriff, you've arrived." Lovett raised a bony finger toward Billy and said, "There, Sheriff Linford, is the man you told me you were looking for. Billy Young from Casper."

Linford moved down the aisle squinting. "Why, I believe it is." As he got closer, he said, "Yes, sir. It certainly is." The sheriff raised himself to his full height. "Young fella, I arrest you for the murder of Jeets Duvall."

"What?" Billy shouted.

"You killed one of my hands, Billy Young," Lovett said in a righteous tone, "and we exact a price for murder in this county."

"Sheriff," Billy said, "you know the circumstances of me killing Jeets. I told you all about it the day I brought in his body.

You didn't say anything about murder then."

Linford seemed to fumble for words.

Lovett answered for him. "The sheriff had not had an opportunity to complete his investigation at that point, Young. Now he has. We know you claim Mr. Duvall had committed some crime, but as the sheriff's investigation shows, you had the man apprehended, but for you, apprehension wasn't enough. Bringing him to trial was not your way. Instead, you took the law into your own hands." Lovett spun on his boot heel and aimed the finger he'd earlier pointed at Billy in the direction of Jill. "Isn't that so, Miss Springer?"

Jill's eyes grew wide, and she jumped to her feet. "No, that's not right. Jeets had already murdered Chester Black—shot him down like a dog." She was fighting tears, but Billy could see it was a losing battle. "He had tried to kill Billy, too. That was his intention, but Billy got the gun away from him before he could. Jeets Duvall was a cold-blooded murderer. Billy only did what any man would've done in the same situation."

Lovett fixed her with his eyes. "When the sheriff questioned you about this, didn't you tell him Billy Young wrapped a rope around Jeets Duvall's neck after the man had already surrendered?"

"Yes, but—"

"Didn't you tell Sheriff Linford Mr. Young lifted Duvall onto a stool?"

"Yes, I did. It was—"

"Didn't you also describe how Mr. Young kicked the stool out from under the man's feet?"

Jill was now in tears. "Yes, yes," she said, "but Billy had already explained all of that to the sheriff the day we came into town. Billy never tried to hide what happened. The sheriff knew all of it, and he said he understood what Billy had done."

"Stop it, Jill," Billy said. "It's all right."

Lovett's shoulders were squared, and his eyes appeared full of life. Linford cleared his throat. "Billy Young, like I said before, I arrest you for the murder of Jeets Duvall." The sheriff lifted his right hand toward the pistol at his hip, but before his fingers touched the leather, Billy's short-barreled Colt was aimed at his heart.

The sheriff's jaw dropped at the speed at which Billy's gun appeared, but he still held his hand next to his holstered Smith and Wesson.

Somewhere in the congregation a woman screamed, but everyone stayed where they were.

"Don't do it, Sheriff," Billy warned, and the sheriff's hand eased down.

Billy stepped forward, took the man's pistol, and tucked it into his own belt. "Now," he said to the crowd, "everyone stay put."

Mrs. Unger, her fine features pinched, started to say something but stopped herself and instead lifted trembling fingers to her lips. Her sad eyes offered him her apology. Billy gave her a smile but expected it looked as empty as it felt, and he followed it up with the same "what-the-hell" shrug he'd seen his brother give every time he was tossed from the back of a bronc.

He stepped over to Mrs. Unger and took the transcript from her. "I reckon I've gone to too much trouble for this to leave it behind," he said and shoved the folded papers into his shirt.

Billy kept his Colt up and watched them as he backed toward the rear of the sanctuary. When he got to the door, he reached behind him for the knob, and as he did, he said to the sheriff, "It may be I could've handled Jeets Duvall in a better way, Sheriff. I've turned it over in my own mind more than once since it happened. But I don't think what I did was murder. You never thought it was murder yourself until this man—" Billy jerked the barrel of his gun toward Lovett. "—convinced you to think it was."

Billy leveled his eyes at Henry Lovett. "And you, sir, I have never met a man like you, but at the same time, you're just like everyone I know. It's a troublesome thing."

Without taking his eyes from the rancher, he said, "I'll shoot the first man who follows me through this door." Billy turned the knob and stepped outside, slamming the door behind him. He shoved the revolver into his holster and sprinted toward his horse. He ripped the reins from the rear of the phaeton and threw his leg over the saddle. Turning the animal toward the river, he didn't spare the spur.

CHAPTER SIXTEEN

A posse of a half-dozen men trailed Billy for a ways back into the mountains, but it didn't seem their hearts were in the chase, and Billy lost them without much effort.

Once he was sure they had given it up, he made camp next to a stream, and with a line and hook he carried wrapped around a small stick in his saddlebag, he caught a couple of nice-sized brook trout and cooked them over a small fire. He rested in the shade. After sunset, he saddled Badger and rode down to the spot on Antelope Creek Jill had told him about. The place was a couple of miles north of Probity and easy to find, but only if a person knew what to look for.

He had set up his second camp of the day and was brushing Badger down when he heard the sound of approaching footsteps in the cottonwoods. He had the Marlin out of its scabbard and leaning against a rock, and he edged over to it and picked it up. A round was already jacked into the chamber, and he pulled back the hammer and dropped to one knee, putting the rock between himself and the oncoming sound.

Whoever was out there made no effort to do it with stealth, which caused Billy to wonder if this might be a trick. He held his breath and listened for quieter movement from other directions but could hear nothing.

The sounds grew louder then stopped altogether. "Billy," someone called out, "it's me." He recognized the voice as Jill's, and he released his breath in a whoosh.

"Come on in, Jill," he said, lowering the Marlin's hammer.

The girl stepped into the clearing, leading one of the horses Billy had consigned to the liveryman to sell for her. If it weren't for her voice, he was not sure he would have recognized her in the dim light. All of her clothes were at least a couple of sizes too big.

When she saw Billy, she dropped the horse's reins and ran to him. As she did, the flop hat she wore, which was maybe *three* sizes too big, toppled to the ground. She threw her arms around him and buried her face into his chest. "Oh, Billy," she cried, "thank goodness, you're safe. I was so scared when you ran out of the church like that." She pulled him closer, and he lifted his hands to her shoulders and laid his cheek against the top of her head.

"I'm all right," he whispered. "There was a posse, but I lost them."

"Henry Lovett is still trying to rile everyone up to find you, and with some folks he's doing a pretty good job of it, too. There are others, though, who figure whatever Jeets Duvall got, he had coming. I heard one man say he doubted Duvall ever did anything in his life he didn't deserve hanging for."

Her words were kind, but Billy knew if the cold facts of the events in the cabin were ever told in a court of law, it would not sound good. "The day my brother was killed," Billy said, "an old friend told me there wasn't a jury in the state that would convict me for killing his murderers. And it may be true that all who knew Jeets would agree he deserved what he got, but even so, I expect if the law wants to push it, and I have to face the charge, it'll not turn out well."

He felt her arms squeeze him tighter. "Don't say that, Billy. Don't even think it."

Billy was not sure how long they stood that way, holding each other in the darkness. It could have been seconds. It could have been minutes. Later, after she was gone, when Billy lay atop his bedroll letting his mind free-range, he smiled to himself and thought they might've stood there for hours. It didn't matter how long it was. During whatever time they held each other, Billy decided Mrs. Unger had been right. Jill Springer had stolen his heart. He was a man falling in love.

Finally, Billy held her out away from him so he could see into her face. "How's Mrs. Unger?" he asked.

"She's safe. She says despite Lovett's denials, everyone in town believes what's written in the transcript is the truth, and there's no chance now Lovett or the others will hurt her. She said even if she was struck by lightning the townspeople would probably think Henry Lovett and his friends had a hand in it."

"That's good," Billy said, but he was not as convinced as Grace Unger was that Lovett was through. Maybe Lovett had given up on the idea of bribing his way into possession of his neighbors' land—and even if he hadn't, the commissioners no doubt had—but Billy could not imagine a man as vainglorious as Henry Lovett letting all of this drop. His plans had been thwarted, and now because of Mrs. Unger and Billy, not only was Lovett unable to drive his neighbors out of business, but those same neighbors would soon be constructing irrigation ditches across his property. Lovett would never forget about that, and, if not today, someday he would exact a price from Grace Unger. Whether she realized it or not, Billy was convinced that was Mrs. Unger's situation.

As far as his own situation, Billy doubted Henry Lovett was willing to wait before exacting a price from him.

He dropped to the ground and leaned against the same rock a few minutes earlier he'd been hiding behind. "Lovett's capable of anything. If he thought he could get away with killing her, he'd do it," Billy said. "And unless he's stopped, he *will* do it someday."

Billy took off his hat and set it aside. He ran his hands through his hair and stretched out his legs. He wanted a break. For just five minutes he wanted to be able to stop thinking about all of this. For five minutes he wanted to forget about his brother lying dead on the prairie. He wanted to forget about putting things back in balance. He wanted to forget about the feelings he felt when he killed Baxter and Duvall and whether something was right or wrong or good or bad. For just five minutes Billy wanted to forget about killing Zeke Blood.

He lifted his head and stared up at the constellations. How far away were those lights, he wondered.

After a bit, the stars were blocked by Jill's bending over him and smiling. "I know you've had a hard day," she said, "but don't you go to sleep. I didn't ride all the way out here to watch you sleep, Billy Young."

Now Billy felt himself smile. That sounded like the sort of thing he used to say to Frank. Billy recalled just before his brother was killed, he'd been giving Frank hell about sleeping on the train.

It was good with Jill in camp. She pulled her baggy pants up, plopped down beside him, and lay her head on his shoulder.

Billy glanced down at her oversized clothes. Once long ago, a traveling circus had come through central Wyoming. They set their tent up by the old fort. The circus had acrobats and jugglers and even a woman who could walk on a wire stretched taut twenty feet above the ground. There had been some fantastic things to see at that circus, but the thing Billy had always remembered the most was a clown who wore a huge, baggy suit. That clown had made ten-year-old Billy laugh so hard he couldn't catch his breath. There was even a moment when Billy thought he was actually going to die. As he gasped with laughter under the big-top tent, he had pictured himself lying in a coffin with a lunatic's smile frozen onto his dead face, and that had made him laugh all the more. Jill's baggy clothes made Billy remember the clown, and he hoped it was dark enough she couldn't see him stifling his laughter now.

"Where did you get those clothes?" he asked.

She lifted her head and gave him a sideways look that made him think maybe she *could* tell he was fighting off a laugh. "I didn't have anything to ride in, so Mrs. Jordan lent me some of her late husband's old things. He was a small man, I guess," she added.

"Maybe he was," allowed Billy, "but not quite small enough, I'd say." He couldn't hold it anymore, and the laughter burst out of him.

She doubled her fist and gave him a whack on the shoulder, but she laughed, too. "I guess it does look pretty silly," she said, wrenching the huge shirt around so it hung better on her narrow frame. When she did, she said, "Oh, my, I almost forgot." She reached into the front pocket of the shirt and pulled out an envelope. "Here," she said, "this telegram came for you at Mrs. Jordan's this afternoon."

"Telegram?" He took it from her and tried to read it but couldn't make out the words in the gloom. He dug into his own shirt pocket, pulled out a wooden match, and struck it on the rock. It flared, and he held the light next to the paper. He read aloud. " 'Caught my culprit. Figured it was time to help you catch yours. I have good news and lots of it. Meet you at the boarding house tomorrow, eight a.m. Signed: Hugo.' "

Billy shook out the match and flicked it away. At first he hated the idea of the deputy becoming involved. Billy didn't want Hugo to see what a mess he had made of things—Zeke Blood was still not caught, and now Billy was accused of murder. But after a second thought, it would be good to have Hugo around.

"What do you suppose he means by good news?" Jill wondered.

Billy smiled. "With Hugo there's no telling. Could be a new whorehouse is opening on Center Street."

"Do you think you should risk coming into town?"

"Probably not. When Hugo shows up in the morning, you give him directions out here. And tell him he'd best call out his name before he steps into my camp. With all his enemies, it'd be a shame if he was killed by a friend."

CHAPTER SEVENTEEN

"Don't shoot, gunman. I got my hands in the air."

Billy knew by the raspy voice it was Hugo Dorling in the bushes. "Come on in, Hugo," Billy called, and the deputy stepped into the clearing, his arms stiff and extended straight up as high as they would go. It looked so ridiculous, it was funny.

"I'm reachin' for the sky, pard," Hugo said. It seemed Hugo had read a dime novel or two himself.

"Get in here, you fool," said Billy, running over to the man. He stuck out his hand and Hugo gave it a shake. Now that he was closer, Billy noticed Hugo was sporting a cut lip, black eye, and swollen ear. "Good God, Hugo, what happened to you?"

"That deacon I was chasin' beat the shit out of me, that's what. I had to shoot the son of a bitch in the knee just to get him caught." Hugo shook his head in disgust. "Who'd ever thought a Baptist could be so damned tough? All-in-all, though," he added, "I look pretty good compared to this fella." He jerked his thumb back over his shoulder, turned, cupped his hand around his mouth, and called out, "Come on in."

Billy heard more rustling in the bushes, and a large man leading two horses walked into the camp. Billy had to look twice, but finally he recognized the man to be young Walter P. Cosgrove. Billy couldn't believe his eyes. "My Lord, Walt, it's you." Billy ran over, grabbed Walter's hand, and shook it with both of his. "Damn, Walter, it's great to see you. I feared you were—" Billy caught himself before he actually said it.

Walt finished the thought for him. "Dead?" he suggested.

Billy smiled and shrugged. "Well, yes, sir, I reckon that's the word I was searching for."

Walt flipped the reins he held around a low-hanging limb. "I damned near was," he said.

The man did not look good. Both of his eyes were blackened. The inside of the right eye was so red it looked as though it had been painted. There were stitched-up cuts all over his face and a long one on the side of his head. Covering his ear was a bandage the size of an apple.

"Well, I want to hear all about it," Billy said, "but first grab your cups and come over by the fire. I got some coffee going."

Both men went to their horses and dug into their bags for their cups. They then squatted around the small fire Billy had built.

Billy poured them each some coffee. "It really is grand to see you, Walt. These're bad men. I figured they had killed you, for sure."

Hugo laughed. "They would have," he said, "if Walter here had been merely a common fella like you or me."

"Stop it, Hugo," Walt said with a smile.

"Come on," said Billy. "What's the story? Tell me what happened."

Walter blew on his coffee and took a sip. "A few minutes after you boys left for the barbershop, I was typing away, and five men came in from the back alley. I'd never seen any of them before. I stood up and started giving them hell for coming in my back door. Well, sir, right in the middle of my tirade, one of these fellas hauls back, makes a fist, and hits me square in the jaw."

"Big mistake," chimed in Hugo.

"It made me angry when he did that, so I picked him up and

heaved him across the room. He crashed into the wall and knocked my diplomas and notary public certificate onto the floor—broke the frames all to hell. That's when the fracas really got going. The first fella seemed to be pretty much out of commission, but three of the other ones came at me full blast. The guy who seemed to be leading the bunch just leaned up against the storeroom door watching it all, kind of like a spectator, you know? He was a strange one. I went around for a while with those other three. After a bit, the one I'd tossed against the wall woke up, and he joined in, too. While this was going on, the one who was the boss stopped watching and started rummaging around on my desk. I saw him pick up the transcript, read a little of it, and shove both copies into his shirt. I tried to stop him, but these other fellas were keeping me too busy. While he was reading the transcript, one of the boys I was fighting called out, 'Give us a hand here, Mr. Blood.' And this fella comes over, pulled out his pistol, and hit me with it." Walt lifted his hand and with an easy touch probed the stitches on the side of his head. "I was out before I hit the floor."

"I'm sorry, Walter, that I brought this on you," Billy said. "I really am."

"Wait a minute," said Hugo. "The story ain't done yet, not by a long shot."

"No, not yet," said Walter. "These fellas dragged me out of my office and hefted me onto a horse and took me out to a field over west of town. By the time we got there, I was pretty much coming around, although I was still a little groggy. They dumped me in this field, and the leader said, 'Kill him.' Just like that he says, 'Kill him. But don't shoot him,' he says. 'It'll make too much noise. Beat him to death.' We were between the oil spur tracks and the river over there a little past the sandbar, and he nodded toward town and said, 'I'll be at the first one of them saloons back yonder having a whiskey. Come and get me when you're done.' And he turned his horse around, and he trotted the couple of hundred yards back over to Center." Walter took another sip of his coffee and stared down into the dark liquid. "He was one cold son of a bitch, that fella was. I gotta tell you."

Up to then Walter had been relating the story in almost school-boy tones, like it all had been some kind of lark. Now, though, his voice turned heavy.

"That was when these fellas started in on me in earnest. Ever since the man hit me with the barrel of his pistol I was not quite myself, and I wasn't putting up much of a fight. I hate to admit it, but those boys were pretty much having their way, and I wasn't doing hardly anything to stop them. But as it happens, it turned out to be my lucky day."

"Lucky day?" Billy looked at Hugo and rolled his eyes.

"Yep, there's no doubt about it. Now we were in that field—you know the one—just behind Center Street, and it turns out there was eight or ten fellas who'd been drinking in one of those saloons. Well, these boys were some wild ones, and they got drunk enough and rowdy enough the bartender kicked them out."

Hugo threw back his head and howled with laughter. "Can you imagine how drunk and rowdy they'd have to be to get kicked out of one of them places? I mean, hell, it ain't like them saloon keepers has a lotta *rules* or nothin'. Christ a' mighty, people get *shot* over there at the rate of two or three a week."

It was obvious Hugo had heard this story a few times, and clearly he enjoyed it.

"Anyway," continued Walter, "when these boys were kicked out of the saloon, they just figured they'd buy a couple of bottles and keep on with their drinking out back. Once they got out back, though, they saw some poor son of a bitch getting the hell beat out of him, and that looked like good sport to them so they sauntered over to have some fun and enjoy the show."

Hugo laughed again and was unable to stop himself from delivering the single-most important piece of information in the whole story. "Turns out them fellas was *fans*," he shouted. *"Fans."* He smacked himself on the knee so hard he sloshed coffee over the back of his hand. "Damn it, shit, *damn*," he cursed, trying to shake the hot coffee off.

"What do you mean they were fans?" Billy asked.

"They were baseball fans," explained Walter. "These fellas are always hanging around the ballpark. They never miss a game."

Hugo, sucking the back of his hand, jumped in again. "When them boys got close enough to recognize the poor bastard gettin' kilt was their hero, the Red Stockin's' star first baseman, Walter P. Cosgrove, the man who's hittin' better'n four hundred this season and so far has twenty-seven homeruns under his belt, they jumped in and beat them four ruffians senseless."

Walter nodded. "That's pretty much it," he said. "They put them down pretty hard. That's for sure. When they were done, they hauled me into town to the doc's, but they left them other fellas out there bleeding in the dirt. I heard a couple of the boys who helped me went back out there an hour or so later and they were gone, so I guess they didn't kill any of them, but from what I was able to make out as I was watching it happen, it looked like they were going to." He shook his head at the memory of it. "It was something."

"Well," said Billy, "that's quite a story. When we got back to your office and saw it torn up the way it was, and you were nowhere to be found, I was plenty worried." He reached over and squeezed Walt's shoulder. "I cannot tell you how glad I am that you're all right."

"He is all right," Hugo said, "but now they've done gone and got him provoked."

Walt looked sheepish. "That's right," he agreed. "That's why I asked Hugo if I could tag along, because these boys have provoked me."

"Provoked, huh?" Billy said with a smile. He sure would hate to have this enormous baseball-playing, court-reporting son of a bitch provoked at him.

Billy refilled their cups with the last of the coffee. "Well, you were right in your telegram, Hugo, when you said you had some good news. Seeing Walter, here, takes a load off my mind."

Billy related to them what he'd learned since he'd last seen Hugo and of the events at the church the previous day, including Lovett convincing the sheriff that Billy had murdered Jeets Duvall.

"Oh, hell," Hugo said, "I wouldn't worry about it none."

"Not worry about it? Are you joking?" That sounded too casual even for Hugo Dorling. "I'm telling you, Hugo, they want to charge me with murder. I had a damned posse chasing me yesterday."

"They ain't gonna charge you with no murder, Billy. Walt's bein' alive is only part of my good news. Another part is rather than chargin' you with murder, they'll be payin' you five hundred dollars instead."

"What?"

"That's right. Seems anytime there's a mail robbery, the federals put out a two-hundred-dollar reward for the robbers. In this situation, the railroad upped the reward to five hundred. Even though there wasn't very much money stole, I reckon the railroad boys back in Chicago figure it's bad for business to have payin' customers and railroad employees shot down in such a brazen fashion." Hugo smiled. "I think it'd be a nice touch if you submitted the forms to collect the reward through the local sheriff's office. After all, it was Linford who saw you haul Duvall's body into town."

Billy felt himself smile, and he had to agree. Using Linford to collect the reward did have the pleasing balance to it that Billy was coming to appreciate.

"While you've been engaged in all your adventures over here," Hugo said, "Walter and me've been busy ourselves. Ain't that right, Walt?"

"Busy as beavers," the big man said.

Hugo finished off the last of his coffee, stood, and crossed to the creek where he stooped to rinse his cup. "You know, Billy, once I discovered that ol' Walter here was still among the livin', him and me got to talkin' about the transcript he'd been workin' on when them fellas barged in on him the way they did so unexpected." He jerked the crown of his big hat in Walter Cosgrove's direction. "Now judgin' just by appearances, you might think Walt is really nothin' more'n a big, none-too-bright first baseman, but as it happens, in Walter's case, appearances are deceivin'. The truth is, the fella's pretty damned smart." A small smile curled the edge of Walt's swollen lip. "He was tellin' me how in the transcript that lawyer, Unger, mentioned that just talkin' about bribin' the commissioners weren't necessarily a crime. To make it a crime, these fellas'd have to do somethin'—" Hugo stopped and searched his memory for a thought that seemed to elude him. After a bit he asked, "How was it you described it, Walt?"

"To make what they did a crime," Walt answered, "according to the law, they'd have to perform some overt act in furtherance of the conspiracy."

Hugo snapped his fingers. "Right," he said. "That's it." He turned back to Billy. "Now, you might be thinkin', Billy Young, that I could make this story go a lot smoother if I just let ol' Walter tell it in the first place, and if you're thinkin' that, you'd be right. But, then again, it ain't my way." He sloshed some water around in his cup. "You probably remember this since you ended up writing it out from the carbon paper, but the example of one of them *overt acts* Unger gave in the transcript was these fellas goin' to the bank the next mornin' and withdrawin' the money. Even if they never did offer the money to the commissioners, just them goin' to the bank to get it would be an act in furtherance of the conspiracy, and they'd be guilty of a crime. Am I right, there, Walter?"

"That's right."

"But," Billy said, "their plan fell apart when they discovered Unger had Bernard Simms writing down their conversation."

"That's true, but Walt here started lookin' at it a little different. He figured—"

Walt, not being a timid man, interrupted. "I figured they did an act to further the conspiracy when they did everything they could to stop what was contained in the transcript from becoming known. Maybe we can't prove they ordered the train robbery, but we can connect them to the break-in at my place through Zeke Blood. Beating me up and stealing twenty or so pieces of paper from my office may not be much of a crime, but," he added with a smile, "the way I see it, they did it in furtherance of a conspiracy."

Hugo jerked his cup up and down in the air a couple of times to flick the creek water from it. "After hearin' what Billy said about Lovett goin' to Unger's house the next mornin' and makin' a threat, I'd say that'd be an overt act, too; wouldn't you, Walt?"

"Sounds like it to me," Walt agreed.

He checked the cup to make sure it was dry. " 'Course, we didn't know nothin' about that until today." He carried the cup over to his horse and tucked it down into his saddlebag. While he was there, he dug out a handful of papers and brought them back to the campfire with him. "Although what Walt said sounded good to me, I didn't really know whether he had this overt act business figured right or not, so I went up to the courthouse and ran the idea by the Deputy U.S. Prosecutin' Attorney. He's a pretty smart fella hisself, but he wasn't sure at first. He figured it was a close call, but he gave 'er some more thought, looked in a couple of books, and in the end he said he'd have to go along with Walter. As far as he was concerned, tryin' to *hide* a conspiracy was the same as trying to *further* a conspiracy. He had Walter come up to the courthouse and sign an affidavit tellin' all the things them fellas had agreed to do in that transcript, and when he was done, the Deputy Prosecutor gave me these." Hugo tossed the papers he'd pulled from his bag over to Billy.

There were nine separate documents. Billy had to look at them awhile to understand what he held. They were all preprinted forms, but each one had a name typed in a blank at the top of the page. The first four of the documents contained the name "John Doe."

"Them 'John Does,' " Hugo explained, "is for the four fellas who busted into Walt's office and beat the ever-lovin' dog shit out of 'im. The next one on the pile there is for your sworn enemy, Mr. Zeke Blood."

Sure enough. The fifth document down had Blood's name at the top. The last four forms contained the names of Henry Lovett, Philip McCutcheon, Arthur Price, and Frederick Cooke.

At the top of each of these nine documents in dark bold print were the words, **"WARRANT FOR THE ARREST OF:"** And at the bottom of each page was the swirly cursive signature of the United States Court Magistrate for the District of Wyoming.

CHAPTER EIGHTEEN

When Billy, Hugo, and Walt stepped through the sheriff's front door, Linford had his boots propped on his desk, and he was reading a two-week-old copy of *Leslie's Illustrated Newspaper.*

"Good day, Sheriff," Billy said. Billy didn't know if the surprise he saw flash across Linford's face was caused by Billy's own brashness at strolling into the sheriff's office or by Hugo staring down at Linford in his usual steely-eyed manner. "I'd like you to meet a couple of friends of mine. This large fella's name is Walter Cosgrove, and this gentleman here is Deputy U. S. Marshal Hugo Dorling."

The deputy's name was a familiar one around Wyoming, and it was well known that he was not a man given to suffering fools. Linford's feet thumped to the floor, and he started to stand but stopped when Hugo said, "Don't bother to get up, Sheriff. This won't take long." Hugo dropped a stack of papers on the corner of Linford's desk and jerked a thumb in Billy's direction. "I hear there's some talk that Billy Young murdered one of your local citizens—a low-life rascally, scoundrel bastard by the name of Jeets Duvall."

"Er-a, why, yes," Linford said. "That accusation's sure been made." He looked toward Billy. "This young fella, by his own admission—"

Hugo held up a hand. "Hold on," he said. He lifted the top two papers from the stack. "Take a look at this." He tossed the documents over.

The first was the notification of reward from the United States Government for the two surviving perpetrators of the mail robbery, and the second was the notification from the railway company increasing the government's reward from two hundred dollars to five hundred.

Linford appeared a bit unsettled but got out, "Well, sir, these are interesting, but they don't list any names. How'm I supposed to know Jeets is one of the men this reward is for?"

Hugo's smile lifted the edges of his mustache, and he leaned across Linford's desk. "The first way you'll know is because Jeets Duvall fits the description of one of the men contained on them papers you're a-holdin'. The next way you'll know is Mr. Young here was a victim of the robbery and saw those men with his own two eyes, and he was as certain as could be the man he was forced to kill that day in the La Prele cabin was one of the murderers who held up the train. If that still ain't good enough for you, we can get sworn statements from both the train engineer and an unfortunate young woman, who, with her now-deceased bridegroom husband, was a passenger that day. They can both describe the killers, and my guess is their descriptions'll match Mr. Duvall down to his toenails."

Linford seemed to give it some thought. "Maybe," he allowed.

"There's also Mr. Simms's watch," Billy added. "It was stolen during the robbery. I took it off of Jeets's body and showed it to you when I brought him in."

Linford gave that some thought as well. After a bit, he made a noise like he was sucking something out of a tooth and swiped a quick glance at the large star pinned to Hugo's vest. Finally, he said, "All right."

"Well, fine," said Hugo, rubbing his hands together and acting as pleased as he could be with the sheriff's good sense. "Now we have them awful unpleasantries out of the way, let's move on to other business." He reached again to his stack of papers, picked them all up, and handed the whole batch over to Linford. He sat in one of the chairs positioned in front of the desk and told Billy and Walt to have a seat as well. "Make yourselves comfortable, boys, while the high sheriff here does his readin'."

Linford scanned the first five forms quickly. When he got past the John Does and Zeke Blood and read the names on the last four warrants, his bushy eyebrows folded together and the ruddiness drained from his face like water from a rusty bucket. "My, God," he said, "you have warrants here for the arrest of—" He looked up at Hugo with rheumy eyes.

Hugo grinned. It was, Billy decided, sinful how much ol' Hugo was enjoying all of this.

"That's right," Hugo said. "We're about to empty Probity's coop of its biggest roosters and use 'em to fill your jail. Now, it is my practice in situations like this to show my respect to local authorities, like yourself, by allowin' them to participate in the arrests. On the other hand, seein' as these fellas are men of prominence in your community, if it'd make you uncomfortable to come along, I'd understand. If need be, me and my deputies here can handle it by ourselves."

Deputies?

Billy didn't recall being sworn in as a deputy. He glanced over at Walt. By the look on Walter's face, he didn't recall it either. Billy guessed little things like an oath of office and a badge didn't mean too much to Hugo.

"Then again," Hugo continued, "next year is an election year, and it could be you'll be seekin' other employment once it gets out that you did not wish to take part in the arrest of arrogant criminals who conspired to bribe your county commissioners and your district judge."

Clearly Sheriff Linford was in a quandary. Hugo let him stew for a while then leaned in closer. In a confidential tone of voice he said, "Let me tell you somethin', Sheriff. We're gonna arrest these fellas for conspiracy. There ain't no doubt about it. Out in his saddlebag, Billy Young here's got a transcript made by a genuine court reporter. It's a transcript of the conversation the four men named in them warrants had while they was doin' the actual conspirin'. We're gonna get 'em. It's just that simple. And there's a chance—although a slim one, I admit—but a chance just the same that we'll be gettin' one or all of 'em for orderin' a train robbery and a series of murders and attempted murders as well. I've been in the law enforcement business a long time, and I can tell you in a situation like this, even though we could do the job without you, it would not go well for any sheriff who refused to assist the office of the United States Marshal." He leaned back in the chair. "While you're givin' all this your consideration, you might add in my earlier point about the im-pendin' election."

Linford stared at Hugo without speaking. He swallowed and glanced down at the warrants. He waited long enough before responding that Billy wondered if the man would ever speak again, but then he let out a little groan, nodded, and whispered, "Okay."

Hugo smacked himself on the knee, stood, and extended his hand to the sheriff. "That's damned gracious of you, Sheriff. Damned gracious. It'll be a pleasure to work with you. It truly will."

Linford shook Hugo's hand but seemed leery.

"What time's it gettin' to be, anyhow?" Hugo asked as he compared his pocket watch to the clock on the wall. "I'm hungry enough for mutton." Seeing it was nearly noon, he suggested they have a bite to eat.

"Nah," said Linford, "you fellas go ahead. I got some paperwork I need to catch up on."

Hugo dashed around the desk, took the sheriff by the elbow, and helped him to his feet. "Ah, hell," he said, "come along. It'll be my treat." It was clear the penny-pinching Hugo did not trust the sheriff enough to leave him alone. "We're partners now. We gotta get to know one another better, right, boys?"

"Absolutely," Walt said.

"Sure thing," said Billy.

Sheriff Linford hung a "Back-in-One-Hour" sign on the door, and the four men walked to Lottie's Café. They were early enough to beat the worst of the noon-time crowd, and they found a table by a front window. Pot roast with boiled carrots was the specialty of the day, and the four men ordered the special. To no one's surprise, it turned out to be a fine meal, and Billy, as was his way, succumbed to his sweet tooth and finished off with a slice of rhubarb pie.

"No pie for me, ma'am," said Hugo to Lottie, "just another cup of coffee." After the coffee was poured and the pie delivered, Hugo looked to Linford and said, "You know these fellas better than we do. What d'you figure would be the best way to take 'em into custody? It'd be nice to do it without anyone gettin' kilt, and, if possible, I'd like to get 'em all at once."

Linford pulled a half-smoked cigar from his shirt pocket and fired it up. "Well," he said, "I don't know when you could catch all of them together, but tonight, and every other Monday night, for that matter, three of them play poker over at Buck's Saloon. Lovett won't be there, but the others always are."

"Poker, eh? What time does the game begin?" Hugo asked.

"About nine o'clock, I'd say."

"Do any of their hands join the game?"

Linford shrugged. "Most times a couple of the boys'll come in to drink a bit and socialize, but they rarely play. The games get a little too steep for cowboy wages."

Billy was disappointed Lovett wouldn't be there. "How come Lovett won't be playing?" he asked. "I thought the four of them always hung together."

"Lovett ain't a gambling man," Linford said. "Says he don't like leaving things to chance."

"These boys gonna give us any trouble?" asked Hugo.

"I don't know," Linford answered. "Artie Price and Phil Mc-Cutcheon both can be bad ones. To my way of thinking, Price is crazy, though he's never shown any signs to violence that I know about, but you never know what he might do. McCutch-eon on the other hand ain't crazy, but he is mean. I figure him to be the real problem. Fred Cooke I expect will offer no resistance at all."

"Well, then," Hugo said with a twinkle in his eye, "you, me, and Billy, here, will handle Mr. Cooke. We'll leave McCutcheon and Price to Walter."

Billy, Walter, and Hugo had a good laugh, but Linford never cracked a smile.

Billy and the others arrived at Buck's a little before nine o'clock, ordered beers, and sat at a table in the corner. Billy felt a flutter in his stomach that he knew would make waiting for something to happen difficult. He was glad they were moving in on at least three of the men who started all of this, but he worried that go-ing after these men first might scare off Zeke Blood before Billy could get at him.

"Most often they play at the last table in the back," Linford said. He nodded toward the rear of the room.

"It ain't a very busy place, is it?" Hugo observed.

"Mondays are 'bout the slowest night of the week. I figure that's why McCutcheon and the others chose Monday for their game. It's quieter and Buck can give 'em better service."

Buck, the owner, was a man in his late forties. Since he wasn't busy, he stood behind the bar chewing on a toothpick and watching the traffic pass by on Main. As he stood there, he opened a large jar, took out a pickled egg, and began eating it. He ate the entire egg without ever pulling the toothpick out of his mouth. Billy mentioned that oddity to the others.

"I reckon I've known Buckley going on twenty years," Linford said, "and I can't recall ever seeing the man without a toothpick in his mouth. He can be eating, smoking, or drinking, it don't matter to him. He's always got a toothpick. I expect that man chews on a toothpick when he's engaged in domestics with the wife."

The bartender pulled another egg from the jar, ate it, and swigged down half a beer, all with the toothpick in place.

"What's wrong with his arm?" Walter asked.

Buck was a big, burly-looking man, whose right arm was thick with muscle, but his left arm was thin, shrunken, and deformed.

Linford blew a plume of cigar smoke at the ceiling and said, "When Buck was young, he was in the army and stationed over at Fort Fetterman. One day they went out on patrol and got into a skirmish with half a dozen Indians and Buck took an arrow in the arm. From what I hear, it damn near killed him. He survived, but his arm was never much use, and after a while it sort of shriveled up to what you see dangling there now. Buck gets along all right, though. He can do about anything, but, boy, I tell you, he don't have any fondness for Indians." He pointed to a sign behind the bar. Printed in large red letters were the words, *NO INDIANS ALLOWED.* "There's that statute, you know, that makes it illegal to serve alcoholic beverages to Indians. Well, sir, as sheriff, I know for sure Mr. Buckley has no problem with turning a blind eye to just about every other law on the books, but I guarantee you, there ain't never been an Indian served a drink in Buck's Saloon, not in its entire history, and there never will be, neither, not so long as it's Buckley behind the bar."

Two men walked through the front door, and Walter stiffened.

"What's the problem, Walt?" Billy asked.

"Those men there," Walter said. "They're two of the ones who came into my office the other day."

Billy and Hugo turned toward the men for a look. Sure enough, they were even more beat up than Walter, but they were armed, and it was clear they still held some fight.

Walter started to stand, and Hugo put a hand on his arm. "Hold on, boy. Let's wait before we make a move."

Walt protested. "But we got our warrants," he said. "Those are a couple of the John Does."

"I know it," said Hugo, "and we'll get 'em, but let's just wait until the others show up. We don't want to scare 'em off." He turned to Linford. "Do you know them fellas?" he asked.

"I don't know their names, but they work for McCutcheon."

The men stood at the bar, and Buck poured them two whiskeys without even bothering to ask what they wanted. They both were beat to hell, but the younger of the two had the worst of it. His lip was cut so bad he had to pull it away from his mouth just to sip his drink.

"Them two fellas skew the odds a bit," Hugo observed, "which ain't good. Usually when the odds're too much against you, you end up havin' to kill someone."

"Sounds all right to me," said Walt. As he was staring at the two men, the muscles in his jaw were doing a little dance.

Billy lifted a hand toward the Remington at Walt's hip. "You ever fire your forty-four in anger, Walter?"

The big man turned to Billy, pursed his lips, and gave his head one quick shake. "But I'm ready to do it, Billy, if I must. Those fellas wanted me dead."

"Let's hope it don't come to that," Hugo said. He started to lift his beer but stopped halfway to his mouth when the three men they waited for came into the saloon.

They were an affable bunch, greeting Buck, the two boys at the bar, and the smattering of other patrons, all of whom they seemed to know.

The largest of the group had to be six-three, and he smacked his hand on the bar as they headed to their regular table. "Bring us our usuals, Buck, if you please, and a fresh deck of cards as well."

"That one's Phil McCutcheon," Linford said. "He can be dangerous. The thin one wearing the coat and string tie is Artie Price. The heftier fella's Fred Cooke."

Buck brought them a tray of drinks and a deck of cards, and the men settled into what appeared to be genial conversation.

"Walter," Hugo said, "you go over to the bar and put yourself between them two fellas there and the three at the table. You watch 'em, and if they try anything when we make the arrest, do whatever is required to stop 'em."

Walt nodded.

"Billy, you, me, and the sheriff here'll go over to the table. You be to my left. Sheriff, you go to my right, and both of you, stay spread out. I'll do the talkin'." He took a deep breath, met each of their eyes, and asked, "Are we ready?" When no one said he wasn't, Hugo said, "All right, boys, let's go."

As they pushed themselves from their chairs, Billy could hear a strange noise in his ears. It was distracting until he decided it was his pounding heart sloshing his blood around with enough force to splash it against his eardrums the way whitewater splashes rocks.

Walt's eyes were set on the two men at the bar, and his expression was determined. Linford appeared scared enough Billy figured if anything happened, the man would prove to be worthless. Hugo was as casual as ever. Once they were on their feet, the deputy took a last sip of his beer and wiped his mustache with the fingertips of both hands. To Billy's surprise, he had a smile on his face.

Hugo was a curious fella. Billy was ready to do this job, but he did not have to check himself in the mirror behind the bar to know he was not wearing a smile.

They crossed the room and halted maybe ten feet from the table where the men sat. Billy positioned himself to where he was looking at Price's left side, full on to Cooke, and more or less to McCutcheon's right. Considering Linford had said the most likely one to try anything would be McCutcheon, Billy was glad to have a good view of the man's right hand and the Smith and Wesson Frontier holstered at his hip. Out of the corner of his eye, Billy could see Walt and the two men at the bar.

"Evenin', gents," Hugo said in an amiable tone.

The three men looked up at him, then to Billy, and finally to the sheriff. "Evening," they responded, but their tone was not as friendly as Hugo's.

Hugo introduced himself. "Name's Hugo Dorling," he said. "I'm with the U.S. Marshal's office."

Cooke had been dealing, and he placed the deck he held on the table.

"I'm afraid I got some bad news for you men," Hugo said. Earlier he had tucked the warrants into his shirt, and they caused his shirt and vest to bulge. He patted the bulge now and said, "I got a warrant here for the arrest of each one of you fellas," and dropped his hand back to his side.

McCutcheon was the first to speak. "You got *what?*" he asked. He turned to the sheriff. "What's this all about, Linford?"

"What the deputy says is true, Mr. McCutcheon," Linford said. "He's got arrest warrants for the three of you signed by the Magistrate out of Casper."

"You got to be joking," said Price. His back was to Hugo, and he turned to his right to stare at Linford.

"What're we being arrested for?" asked Cooke.

"For conspiracy to bribe elected officials," Hugo answered. "And for questionin' regardin' the theft of United States mail. I expect you'll be asked some questions about a few other things, too, before we're done."

Billy could see everyone in the saloon was turned to watch the show except for Walter Cosgrove. He had his back to them, facing the two at the bar.

"Now, I'll ask you fellas to stand and lay whatever firearms you're totin' on the table there. I'll then ask you to accompany us over to Sheriff Linford's jail."

McCutcheon leaned back in his chair, balancing it on its two rear legs. "You must be out of your Goddamned mind."

Hugo gave a little laugh. "Well, sir," he said, "that may well be. There's those who've suggested it before you. But crazy or not, I'll be takin' you gentlemen in." He dropped his voice to a raspy whisper, but it was still plenty loud enough for everyone in the room to hear. "One way or the other," he added. "Now stand and lay down your weapons."

There was at least a full minute where no one spoke. Hugo had his eyes leveled at McCutcheon, but Billy could tell the old deputy was watching the other two as well.

After a bit, Fred Cooke stood, lifted his piece, and placed it next to the cards. "We'll be wanting a message delivered to our lawyer," he said, "telling him what's happening."

"The last I heard," said Hugo, "your lawyer was dead—kilt while out a-huntin'." Cooke flinched when Hugo said that. "You'll be welcome, though," Hugo added, "to send a message to whoever you please once you're locked up." He turned his attention to McCutcheon and Price. "You other two, do as your friend here. Place your guns on the table."

Price stood. His back still to Hugo, and without turning, he lifted the long tails of his suit coat, showing he wore no weapon.

McCutcheon slowly came out of his chair, but he made no move to place the Frontier on the table. Instead, he locked eyes with the deputy.

"I'm waitin'," Hugo said, and Billy was certain he saw that curious smile he'd noticed earlier flicker again at the edges of Hugo's eyes. When he saw the smile, it became clear to Billy that Hugo Dorling was enjoying this confrontation. The possibility of bloodshed hung in the air like smoke, but even so, Hugo was having himself a fine ol' time.

When McCutcheon still made no move, Hugo's body tensed, but his right hand relaxed. The movement was almost imperceptible, but Billy saw it. The fingers of Hugo's hand opened just a little.

"I am still waitin'," Hugo said. In a steady and frosty voice he added, "I will kill you, mister." And there was not a doubt in Billy's mind—nor, he was sure, in the mind of anyone else—that Hugo Dorling spoke the truth.

McCutcheon's eyelids flickered, and when they did, Billy knew the man was finished. "All right," McCutcheon said. "I'm gonna put it on the table."

"Fine," said Hugo. "Do it by grabbin' the butt with the tips of your fingers, and lift it out slow."

McCutcheon did.

With that, Billy felt the crashing water in his head ease up a bit, and he gave himself permission to breathe.

"Good," Hugo said, "now you and Mr. Cooke come out from behind the table. Billy, you get in back of 'em, and we'll head over to the jail."

"I hope you've enjoyed your job as sheriff," McCutcheon said to Linford, " 'cause it ain't gonna last much longer."

Linford didn't respond but rubbed the back of his neck and

187

looked at the floor.

McCutcheon and Cooke started around the table, and as they did, McCutcheon said to Hugo, "And, you son of a bitch, I'll have your job, too, before I'm done."

"Now, now, Mr. McCutcheon," Hugo scolded, "don't you know it's rude to be callin' a man a son of a bitch even if he is one? And as far as my job's concerned, why, hell, I was hopin' to find another, less demandin' line of work anyhow."

When McCutcheon and Cooke were around the table and parallel with Price, Price, who had, until then, kept his back to Hugo, pivoted left, and as he turned around, he tossed back his coat with his left hand and brought his right hand to his chest. As the coat flew back, Billy saw the flash of a shoulder holster and Price's hand cover the butt of a pistol.

Billy reached for his Colt and had already cleared leather while the barrel of Price's gun was still inside his coat. In one fluid move, Billy cocked the hammer as he raised his weapon, but before he could level it at Price, he heard a blast. A hole appeared in the front of Price's white shirt and an explosion of gore blew out from his back. Price spun and crashed face-first onto the table, sending drinks, cards, and pistols flying.

Billy looked to Hugo, who stood staring down at the dead man, blue smoke swirling from the muzzle of his gun.

There was a noise to Billy's right, and he turned in time to see one of the two men at the bar reaching for his pistol. But before he could draw, Walter Cosgrove wrapped his huge hand around the man's face and smashed the back of his head down into the bar. The man dropped to the floor, either unconscious or dead. Billy figured it could go either way.

Walter turned to Billy and smiled.

Before Billy could warn him, the second man, the one with the busted lip, picked up a whiskey bottle by the neck and swung it like a club against the side of Walter's head. There was a loud clunk when it hit, and although the thick glass didn't shatter, where the bottle came in contact with Walter's skull, there was a circular break with cracks stellating out from its center. The bottle struck Walt in the same spot he'd been hit before, and his already-stitched-together scalp popped open, sending a sheath of scarlet cascading down the side of his face.

Billy pivoted toward the man with the bottle and leveled his forty-five at his chest. "Drop it and put your hands on the bar," he shouted between clenched teeth. His finger ached to pull the trigger. In his mind he could already see the bastard jerk when the bullet struck. With some effort, he held the finger steady.

When he was hit, Walter had been staggered, but he'd not gone down. He raised himself erect and extended a hand toward Billy, telling him to hold his fire.

The man with the bottle was big and hard-looking, but Billy could see he was little more than twenty. Earlier he'd been too frightened to move when he was looking into the barrel of Billy's Colt. Now the man seemed to get control of himself, and he dropped the bottle. Still it didn't break. It spun in a lazy circle and rolled against a chair.

The man turned his gaze from Billy to Walter, raised his hands, and gave Walt a look as if to say "you'll get no more trouble from me," but Walter would not have it. Despite the man's surrender, Walt drew back his fist and smashed it into the man's jaw, hitting him hard enough to lift his boots off the floor. The man landed in a motionless heap beside his partner.

When it was clear neither of these fellas would be getting back up, Walter turned toward Billy and leaned against the bar. He shook his bloody head in disbelief. "I don't understand it," he said, "but these people *keep* provoking me."

CHAPTER NINETEEN

Buck, the bartender, volunteered to inform the mortician of Arthur Price's death. The rest went in the opposite direction toward the jail. The two John Does, who turned out to be a couple of brothers from Kansas named Bodine, were dragged half the way by McCutcheon and Cooke. The brothers had worked for McCutcheon for a little less than a year. The one who had hit Walt with the bottle regained consciousness after a block or so. When he came to, Hugo made him drag his brother the rest of the way.

A door led from the sheriff's office into a small room that contained a cot, table, and a chair. On the back side of this room was another door leading into the jail.

There were a dozen cages in the cell block—six to a side— with a narrow aisle between them. Each cage measured five feet wide, by six feet deep, by seven feet high. The prisoners were loaded into four of the cages, and each cage was locked by Hugo. Hugo tossed the keys to Linford. "There you go, Sheriff," Hugo said. "Now, if you would, fetch the doctor so he can tend to Walter and these other fellas here." He waved his arm in the direction of the two busted-up Bodine brothers.

Linford nodded and glanced over to Walter, who was leaning against a wall. "You're looking a little peaked, there, young fella. Maybe you better lay down for a while." He led Walt into the small room between the cell block and the outer office. Walt dropped onto the cot, and Linford left for the doctor.

McCutcheon had been quiet ever since Hugo had killed Price, but now he started in again. "You know you'll never make any of this stick, don't you, you bastard?"

Hugo scratched the back of his head. "You know somethin', mister? I think I'm about tired of you callin' me impolite names." He reached into the cell, took McCutcheon by the front of his shirt, and jerked him forward into the bars so fast the man didn't have time to get his hands up to lessen the blow. His face smashed into the steel, and he staggered back onto his cot.

Hugo fixed the big rancher with a scornful glare. "Let me tell you somethin'," he said. "Your party's over. It ended tonight. We got four more to round up." He looked at the conscious Bodine brother. "You," he said, "we know you and your brother was two of the fellas that busted into Walter Cosgrove's office over in Casper the other day."

"I don't know what you're talking about," Bodine said, or at least that's what Billy thought the man had said. His jaw looked to be broken where Walt had hit him, and his words were a jumbled slur.

Hugo ignored the man's denial. "We know Lovett's man, Zeke Blood, was one of the others who was with you. Who're the other two and where can we find 'em?"

Bodine's eyes were glassy, and he appeared to be in enough pain that he was having a hard time following Hugo's question.

Fred Cooke moved to the front of his cage and said, "We don't know anything about anyone busting into that fella's office."

"Nor would you admit it if you did, right?"

"I can tell you, though," continued Cooke, "there were a couple of fellas who used to run with these boys. Their name was Dickens. They also worked for Phil, and they were also brothers. From what I hear, the four brothers got into a fight with each other a few days back. The Dickens brothers got the worst of it, and once they were able to ride, they left. Far as I know, no one knows where they headed off to. They just left. They were real beat up, though—hurt bad. One of them was still puking blood the day they rode out."

Hugo stared at the man for a bit, taking his measure. Billy believed about half of what Cooke said, and he figured Hugo felt the same. Cooke was lying when he said he knew nothing about the break-in at Walter's office. That was plain. And he was lying about the four brothers fighting one another, but Billy figured he was telling the truth about the Dickens boys being hurt. Billy suspected the two coyotes really had sneaked off somewhere to lick their wounds.

"What about Lovett?" Hugo asked.

"What about him?"

"This whole mess was his idea, weren't it? You and this blowhard over yonder—" He jerked a thumb at McCutcheon. "—and even the crazy fool back at the saloon had nothin' to do with the plannin' nor the executin' of the plan neither one. You just went along with Lovett. Ain't that true?"

Cooke squinted at Hugo through the bars. "You know, Mr. Dorling, I reckon I've made about as many mistakes in my life as the next man, but I've never done anything I didn't think to be right. Whatever we did, we had our reasons. If you think you can prove something against us, have at it, but you'll not get me to speak ill of Henry Lovett. He's tough, and he's severe, but he is a fine man. If I say so myself, we're all fine men. That fella you killed back at the saloon may've been foolhardy, but he was my friend, and he too was a fine man. The next talkin' I do'll be to a judge and a jury, and we'll see who's right."

"Okay," Hugo said, "I reckon that's what we'll do." He turned and started for the door. "Come along, Billy, let's get out to the

Lovett place. We got us another couple-a cages to fill before the sun rises."

"Don't count on it, son of a bitch," McCutcheon said. He stayed out of reach toward the back of his cell when he said it.

"I'll either put Lovett in a cage or a coffin," Hugo replied.

"It'll be you who'll fill the coffin, Dorling," said McCutcheon. "Zeke Blood'll shoot your eyes out. And once you're dead, I promise you, Linford ain't gonna have no stomach for this. We'll be home for breakfast."

CHAPTER TWENTY

Billy unhooked his canteen from his saddle horn and had a long drink. He and Hugo were better than a mile from the Lovett place, and it was still awhile before there would be any confrontation, but the sound in his ears of water crashing over rocks he'd heard earlier at Buck's Saloon was already back, and even though he carried a river around inside his skull, Billy's mouth was as dry as dirt.

"I got a bit of a thirst myself," Hugo said, and Billy offered him his canteen. Hugo returned Billy's offer with a grimace. Instead of taking the water, he reached behind him, dug down into his saddlebag, and came out with a fifth of liquor. He pulled out the cork, tossed back a slug, and handed it over to Billy.

Billy turned the bottle so the light of the full moon would hit the label better. "Damn, Hugo, this is Kentucky sipping whiskey."

"Nothing but the very best for me and my friends," Hugo said, although Billy knew that was a lie. Many times he'd watched Hugo and his father sitting at the Young kitchen table drinking the kind of rotgut that would've cost lesser men their vision.

Billy threw back a jolt of the whiskey, and it sent a pleasant fire through his innards. He recorked the bottle and handed it back to the deputy. Hugo had another drink before he tucked the bottle away.

"It's been a long day, and I could gladly kill that soldier,"

Hugo observed, "but it wouldn't do to enjoy too much of Kentuck's finest before encounterin' a man like Zeke Blood."

Billy thought back to the speed with which Hugo had killed Artie Price at the saloon earlier in the evening. "This may be a dumb question, Hugo, since you're sitting here atop your horse breathing and drinking whiskey, but did you ever go up against a man who was faster than you?"

"Faster? You mean faster at drawin' and shootin'?"

"Yes, sir."

Hugo shifted in his saddle, made himself more comfortable, and answered, "Well, Billy, I'd have to say that as a rule if I knew a man was a better gun hand than me, I wouldn't go up to him direct and say, 'Okay, fella, it's off to the jailhouse with you.' I'd do somethin' by stealth, if possible—get him while he was sleepin'. Or else use trickery—maybe crawl up behind him and whack him with a hunk of lumber or somethin'. That's if I knew he was faster. There are times, of course, when you don't know much about the man you have to face. It's them times that tend to make a fella edgy."

"I guess you've just been lucky then. Every time you've faced someone you didn't know about, like tonight at the bar, for instance, it's turned out you've been faster."

"Tonight don't really count for much. That fella was wearing a shoulder holster. Only the world's biggest fool would try to come out fast from a shoulder holster. But no, sir, to answer your question, I have faced men who were faster. I got a scar on my leg and another on my side, and both of them scars was made by fellas who was considerable faster at pullin' a gun out of a holster than me. Turned out, though, they wasn't as good a shot. Fillin' your hand comes first in gunfightin', but in importance, compared to accuracy, it comes in a distant second." Hugo pulled his makings from his pocket and rolled a cigarette.

They were riding just above the bank of the North Platte, and as Billy listened to Hugo, he watched the low, fat moon's reflection dance along the water.

Hugo popped a match alight with his thumbnail, lit his cigarette, and blew out the flame with a stream of smoke. "I reckon you're askin' me all these questions with Zeke Blood in mind. Am I right?"

Billy nodded. He wasn't sure Hugo had seen him nod, but as it happened, Hugo knew the answer whether he saw Billy nodding or not.

"My guess is you can't pull a sidearm faster than Blood, Billy Young, and I wouldn't count on him bein' a poor shot, neither. We already know the man's a fine shot from what he did to the trainmen at the robbery."

"It's my intention to see him dead, Hugo, but I'd be willing to let the hangman do the killing, if it should turn out he and Lovett decided to surrender without a fight. Do you think they will?"

"I doubt Blood will," answered Hugo. "I never met the man, but I've met a hundred like him. As far as Henry Lovett's concerned, he might give 'er up if his man Blood did. But he's hired Blood to perform certain chores, and he'll expect the man to perform 'em, or die tryin'."

That was one of the things about all of this Billy couldn't understand. "Do you think Zeke Blood is willing to die just because he's hired out to Lovett?"

"First off, I doubt Blood would be willin' to die for anything. But that's just it. He don't expect to die, not in no gunfight anyhow. It would take a lot of convincin' to make a man like Blood even recognize he *can* be killed. Hell, I'm sure he don't even believe such a man might exist who *could* kill him. Second of all, him workin' for hire don't mean squat. He don't have any particular loyalty to Henry Lovett nor anyone else."

"So why does he do it?" Billy asked.

"Why? Hell, boy, you know why he does it—for the pleasure of it. That's why." *The pleasure of it.* There it was again.

"He does it for the pure-dee, hot-damn excitement of it." Hugo added.

Billy had tried to convince himself whatever good feelings he'd gotten from killing Baxter and Jeets Duvall had been because he was exacting justice. But despite Hugo's earlier explanation of certain unlucky men being forced into the darker places, Billy wondered if the feelings he took away from those killings were wrong. Now Hugo was again talking about the *pleasure* of it, and it didn't seem to Billy that Hugo's description of killing had anything to do with justice.

It was a hard thing to figure—and so was Hugo. Billy allowed the topic to drop.

They rode for a bit in silence. Hugo finished his cigarette and right away rolled another. The trail they were riding more or less followed the meanderings of the North Platte, and at one point, as they came around a bend and over a small rise, Hugo reined in.

"What is it?" Billy asked.

Hugo flicked his smoke into the river. The night was quiet enough Billy could hear the hiss the cigarette made as it hit the water.

Hugo lifted his arm toward a stand of trees. "The way them cottonwoods grow right up to the trail down yonder, I don't like it."

"You don't like it? What's not to like? It's just a bunch of trees."

"Seems a good spot for a man with a rifle to be waitin'." He looked at the moon. "If it wasn't so damned bright out tonight, it wouldn't matter so much, but I'd say we make a couple of pretty fair targets."

At first, Hugo's alarm gave Billy the spooks, but Hugo's concern didn't make any sense. The lawman was just being jumpy. There was no way Lovett or Blood could know they were coming, and he pointed that out to Hugo.

Hugo nodded at Billy's logic. "I reckon you're right," he said. "How could they know?" And they both gave their mounts a little spur.

But they hadn't gone a half-dozen steps when it was Billy who drew rein. "They couldn't know—" He looked out into the blackness of the trees. "—unless Linford didn't go for the doc, after all, but rode out here instead."

Billy could see the older man's eyes widen. "Let's leave the trail," Hugo shouted. When he said it, he jerked his horse's head to the left, and as soon as he did, a bullet slammed into the upper right side of Hugo's chest. Even as what had happened registered in Billy's mind, he heard the rifle blast that had sent the bullet into Hugo. Hugo's horse reared and Badger spun. It was good he did, because Billy heard the high-pitched *ffft* of a bullet split the air just above his ear. If the gray hadn't whirled, the shot would have caught Billy right at the forehead.

Despite being struck by the round and his horse's action, Hugo was still mounted, and Billy grabbed Hugo's reins and shouted, "Hang on." He put himself between Hugo and the shooter and lay low over Badger's back. They left the trail in a gallop, and the big gray extended his neck and tucked his ears back. As they ran, Billy heard at least two more shots, but neither man nor animal was hit, and they made it to another line of trees a hundred and fifty yards away.

Once they were in the cover, Billy jumped from his horse and ran to Hugo.

"Jesus Christ, Hugo," he screamed as he hefted the man down from his saddle. *"Jesus Christ,"* he kept repeating. Billy carried Hugo to the base of a tree and laid him down. Freshets of bright red pumped from the hole in Hugo's chest, and Billy knew if he didn't get the bleeding stopped there was no hope. He ripped open Hugo's shirt, pulled out the blood-soaked warrants, and tossed them aside. He jerked off his own vest and folded it in such a way it covered both the dime-sized hole in front and the dollar-sized hole in back. Reaching down, he pulled the belt from Hugo's pants and wrapped it around the vest and shoulder. He gave the belt a jerk, cinching it as tight as he could, and when he did, Hugo let out a yell.

"Damn, son," Hugo gasped, "ain't it bad enough I got a couple of holes in me without you dislocatin' my shoulder?" He shook his head as if to clear it and said, "Help me against this tree trunk." He tried to push himself up but couldn't do it alone.

"I don't know, Hugo," said Billy. "I think you should just lay flat and try to keep still. We got to stop that bleeding." Hugo spat a wad of something dark into the grass and gave Billy a nasty look.

"All right, Goddamn it," Billy said. "Poppa always said you were the stubbornest son of a bitch on two legs." He put his hands beneath Hugo's armpits and propped him against the tree.

Hugo groaned and gritted his teeth. "Shit, kid," he said, "you could be a little bit gentle. I ain't no bale of hay, you know." The old deputy let out a long, raspy breath and wiped the sweat from his forehead with the back of his hand. When his breathing was more or less regular, he said, "Do you remember a little bit ago what I said about them times when you're either unsure of your rival's skills, or if you know he's better, that's the time to use trickery and stealth?"

Billy said he remembered.

"Well, boy, you just got a good example of Mr. Blood usin' those wiles on us. I suggest you do the same. Do not head straight at that man. Do you hear me?"

Billy nodded and looked out across the clearing toward the stand of trees where the shooter had been. "Do you figure it's just him, Hugo, or do you think Linford and Lovett are out there, too?"

"It's just him. He wouldn't expect to need no help on a simple snipin' job like this one. Besides, Lovett wouldn't want to dirty his hands with it, and Linford ain't got the craw."

"So do you figure they're at the ranch house waiting for him to come back and report that he's killed us?"

"That's my guess," Hugo said.

Billy stood and crossed to Hugo's roan. He took the man's Winchester from the scabbard and untied the bags and canteen from the saddle. He brought them back to where Hugo sat against the tree. "Here," he said, placing the items beside the man, "you may need these before I get back."

Hugo thanked him and lay the rifle across his lap.

"Don't you die while I'm gone, Hugo."

The deputy closed his eyes and leaned his head against the tree. "That ain't my plan," he said in a tired voice Billy could barely hear.

The trees thinned out between where Billy left Hugo and the trail leading to the Rocking L. There wasn't much cover, and he was sure Blood could see him, but that was all right. The killer couldn't get off a clean shot, and Billy wanted Blood to know he was headed for the ranch. That way he'd have to follow, and Billy could lead him away from Hugo.

Even though the trees were thinner, they were still thick enough to make the progress slower than Billy liked, but it was necessary until he could make his way back to the trail. Once he was on the trail, he could give the gray his head and be at the ranch in a matter of minutes. Blood would have to stick to the trees for fear Billy would have the same surprise for him he'd planned for Billy and Hugo.

Billy gave the idea of an ambush some thought. It held temptation, but in the end he decided against it. If it came to shooting, despite Hugo's good advice, he wanted to be close enough to see Blood's face.

Billy and Badger broke from the trees and hit the trail. When they did, Billy started to apply the spur, but right away he realized he didn't have to. The big gray's heart was in it, and when the path opened, Badger started to run in earnest on his own.

They passed through the Rocking L's gate less than two minutes later, and Billy didn't pull rein until he was in the yard in front of the house. He leapt out of the saddle while Badger was still moving. He let the reins dangle and slapped the big horse on the rump. The animal trotted around the back of the house toward the barn where he no doubt smelled fresh water.

Billy ran up the porch steps, and before he got to the door, it flew open.

"Did you get 'em, Zeke? Did you kill the—" It was Linford. When he saw the man racing toward him was not Zeke Blood but Billy Young, he reached for his sidearm, but he was much too slow. Billy drew his Colt as he ran, and in a wide sweeping arc, brought the barrel down hard across the side of Linford's head. The man rolled back into the house's parlor where he came to rest against the legs of a table. There was a gash from his hairline to his left eye, and it leaked blood onto the flowered carpet.

Billy rushed into the room right behind Linford's careening body. Lovett, who had been sitting in a chair next to the table where Linford stopped, jumped to his feet. He was armed but made no move for his weapon. Billy ran to him, grabbed him by the front of his shirt, and lifted him to his toes. He shoved the muzzle of the forty-five under Lovett's nose and said between clenched teeth, "You'll do as I say, or your brains'll be dripping from that fancy wallpaper behind you."

The man's eyes bulged to the size of a hen's eggs. He swallowed and nodded. Billy pulled the man's pistol and shoved him back into the chair.

Linford was still out cold. Billy took his gun, too, and lifted him into the chair across from Lovett. There was a lamp on the table between them, and Billy lowered its wick, turning the light to a dim glow.

Lovett, who'd been without words only a moment before, regained his voice. "I don't know what you've got in mind, but I suggest you forget it."

Billy pulled back a curtain and looked toward the gate. Zeke Blood was coming. His dust rose silver in the bright moonlight.

Lovett went on. "You're a tenacious young man, I gotta say. If you'll let this whole ugly mess come to an end, Mr. Young, I promise to make it worth your while."

Billy dropped his Colt into its holster. He crossed the room, pulled Lovett from his chair, and plowed his fist into the older man's gut. Lovett made no noise but fell to his knees in front of Billy, making silent retches and gags. Billy grabbed a handful of white hair and lifted the man's head back. "Never—*never* speak to me again, you son of a bitch. Do you understand me? Not another word, ever."

Lovett didn't answer, but Billy could tell by his expression that he understood.

"You will say only what I tell you to. In about thirty seconds, Blood is going to come onto the porch out there." Billy nodded toward the open front door. "When he does, call out to him and tell him to come in. I will be right behind you. If you do one thing to warn him, I will send a bullet through your skull." Billy didn't bother to ask this time if Lovett understood.

He shoved the man into his chair, walked behind him, and vanished into the room's shadows. "Make it convincing," Billy whispered, as he heard the jingle of Zeke Blood's bit and the creak of saddle leather as he dismounted.

There was the sound of boot heels on the porch, and then Blood filled the doorway. He stopped, peeled a glove from his right hand, and looked into the room.

Lovett cleared his throat and said, "Zeke, come on in." Billy noticed the clever Lovett, unlike Linford, was not fool enough to ask if he had killed them. Lovett still held out hope he would get through this unsullied. "We were just having a drink," Lovett added.

The white of Blood's shirt reflected the dim lamplight. Billy could even see a slight gloss to the killer's black leather vest. He tucked the glove into the gun belt strapped low along his hip.

Blood took a step into the room, his eyes never stopping in any one place. "The young one got away," he said. "He headed in this direction."

"We, uh—we haven't seen anything," said Lovett.

Blood took another step. He was now full in the faint circle of amber light cast by the lamp. Billy stepped from his shadow, the forty-five leveled at Zeke Blood's chest.

To Billy's surprise, the gunfighter smiled.

"Well, now," he said, pushing his hat up a notch on his forehead, "this is convenient. I was afraid I was going to have to spend my entire night checking the outbuildings and looking behind every tree down by the river just so I could find you and kill you."

"You seem not to notice that I have something aimed in your direction."

Blood squinted at Billy. "Is that a shooter you're holding? Why, hell, boy, in this low light, I figured it was a lollipop." He smiled a big square-toothed smile—the same smile he'd given

Billy a week before when he'd spoken of playing poker with a pinochle deck.

"It's been my experience in the short time since making your acquaintance, Mr. Blood, that you like things weighted heavy to your side."

"That's the truth, young fella, I do."

"That's not the way it is now, is it?"

"Oh, I don't know," said Blood. "True, you're holding your weapon and mine's in leather. But there are things on my side as well."

Billy forced himself to return the big man's smile. It wasn't easy, and it felt awkward. "Like what?" he asked.

"For one, you don't know how quick I am. I might be so fast I could whip out my pistol and put one betwixt your eyeballs before you could say howdy-doo."

Billy waggled the Colt. "I doubt it."

The gunfighter continued. "And, too, I know and you know as well, that you have never gone against a real man. You killed some saddle trash, but it doesn't really count, now, does it? Also, I expect you, being callow in the ways of killing, have had to ask yourself some questions over the course of the last few days regarding certain feelings taking another man's life brings about."

Billy was through talking. "Unbuckle your gun belt, Blood, and let it fall to the floor."

Blood ignored the order. "And I reckon," he went on "—and it is just a guess, mind you—you have yet to fully answer those pesky questions to your own satisfaction."

"Put your right hand in the air and unbuckle the belt with your left."

"Plus, if it came right down to a fight," Blood said, "you standing there aiming your shooter and me with mine still holstered would not hardly be fair. And if by some lucky chance

you did kill me without me killing you—an unlikely possibility—you'd have to deal with the unfairness of that for the rest
of your days."

"I'm waiting, Blood, for you to put it down or draw. Those
are your choices."

It was then Billy asked himself why he was giving Blood any
choice at all. It had been his plan to kill the man as soon as he
saw him. Why hadn't he done it the second Blood appeared in
the door? And as fast as the question came, so did the answer.

He didn't because he wanted to so badly.

"If you think I'll be holstering my weapon to make things
equal, you're mistaken," Billy said. "I'm not a man much
concerned with fairness. You're welcome to draw, if you're a
fool. If you decide not to draw, I'll watch you unbuckle your
gun belt and let it fall to the floor. Once you've done that, I'll
take you to Probity to hang. If you don't draw or disarm, I will
kill you where you stand."

Billy felt himself smile once more. This time, though, to his
surprise, the smile was not forced. It was real, and it came easy.
Having Blood at the end of his weapon felt good.

It balanced things.

And with that balance, an expression skittered across Blood's
face that told Billy the killer saw in Billy's smile what he was up
against.

It was then Billy heard himself add the honest truth. "I will
kill you, Mr. Blood, and I'll do it with pleasure."

When he said it, Billy's voice held a sound even he didn't
recognize, and the words caused something to shift in the
gunman's eyes.

"You ain't got the stuff," Blood said, but there was a waver
beneath his bravado that had not been there a moment before.
Something inside Zeke Blood had lost its footing and slipped.

"Think what you want and do what you will. It's all the same to me." But this time Billy was lying. He was willing to take the man to the hangman, but what Billy wanted most was for Blood to pull his gun.

But he didn't. Blood's gaze was locked on Billy, but these were not the steely eyes Billy had seen that afternoon at the train. These eyes were large and wet. And slowly they filled with . . . with what? Billy wondered. And then he knew. He watched as Blood's eyes filled with desperation.

As the desperation took hold, Blood's right hand lifted, and his left hand dropped to his buckle.

CHAPTER TWENTY-ONE

Billy sloshed some water in Linford's face, which caused him to stir, and he took the three men outside. Across the yard at the bunkhouse, there were a half-dozen hands milling about in their long johns and stocking feet. Having heard two riders arriving late at night had brought them out to see what was happening. At first Billy wondered if they might try something, but he informed them he was a Deputy United States Marshal making arrests. On that one, even Billy was unsure if he was telling the truth, but these men were cowboys, nothing more, and none chose to interfere.

Billy ordered a couple of the hands to hitch a team to a buckboard. While they did, Billy took Lovett, Linford, and Blood and tied each of their hands together. Once that was done, he looped a long rope around all three of their necks, and tied the end of the rope to the buckboard.

"It's only three miles back to town," Billy said. "You boys should be able to trot that far. It'll be the last exercise you'll get for a long while."

Billy brought Badger around and tied him to the back of the buckboard as well. He then climbed in the driver's seat and snapped the reins. He was in a hurry to return to Hugo, so he maintained a smart pace.

As might be expected, Badger had less trouble keeping up than did the prisoners.

Billy left the trail where Blood had ambushed them, and

crossed the hundred-and-fifty-yard open space at an even faster clip than he had the mile they'd covered between there and the Rocking L. Linford and Blood screamed protests at the speed they were being forced to run, but Lovett was silent. Billy suspected the man remembered Billy's admonition about never speaking to him again.

The light was dimmer in the trees, and the first time Billy drove by, he must have passed within twenty feet of Hugo without seeing him. He had to back-track twice before he found the spot where he'd left the wounded man. When he brought the buckboard to a stop, the three men tethered behind folded to the ground in a heap.

Billy jumped from the wagon and ran to the tree. Hugo was no longer propped against the trunk but had fallen to the side, his face buried in the grass. The awkward bandage Billy had applied to Hugo's wound was twisted and shone dark in the leaf-filtered moonlight.

When Billy had passed in the buckboard, Hugo had not called out, and now as Billy approached, the old deputy didn't stir. Even in the dim light, Billy could see the flesh along the side of Hugo's face was sallow and waxen.

Billy stopped, unable to force himself to go any closer. "Hugo?" he called. "Hugo, are you all right?" Still there was no response, and Billy told himself no matter how much he called to his friend, there would be no answer.

"Oh, God, Hugo," Billy whispered. His knees turned to sand, and he sunk to the ground a dozen yards from where Hugo lay.

He was not sure how long he sat there, staring down at the colorless grass. After a bit he pushed himself to his feet. He walked over, picked up Hugo's rifle, and returned to the buckboard. Holding the gun, he looked at Zeke Blood. The man lay on his side, his chest heaving.

One round from Hugo's Winchester was all it would take.

Billy was in the process of putting things into balance, and he turned over in his mind how much balance killing Blood with Hugo's rifle would provide. He was still contemplating the symmetry of that idea when he heard the rustle of something behind him.

He looked around to see Hugo pushing himself up against the tree. He was holding the now-empty bottle of Kentucky whiskey. The deputy's bushy eyebrows moved up and down as he tried to bring Billy into focus. "Is that you over yonder, Billy Young?" Hugo asked. There was a noticeable slur to the old man's speech.

Billy felt his insides leap. He wanted to run to the old bastard, but instead he stood his ground. "Yep, Hugo, it's me," he said.

"Well, it's about damned time," Hugo said. "Care for a snort?" he asked.

"I would, Hugo, but from where I stand you appear to've drunk up all you had."

Hugo held the bottle up for closer inspection. "Why, hell, I believe you're right." He tossed it away. "Your bad luck, I reckon. Come over here and help me up. Bein' shot makes it hard to walk."

"You're shot," Billy said, "but it's more than a bullet hole keeping you from walking."

"Well, whatever it is," Hugo said, "come over here and give me a hand. I got better things to do than lean against a tree and bleed."

Billy left Hugo sleeping in the back of the buckboard while he hauled Lovett, Linford, and Blood into the jail. Since Linford had never gone for medical help, once Billy locked the three prisoners up, he would take Walt and Hugo to the doctor's. After the doc tended to them, Billy would send him back to see to the Bodine brothers.

Lovett was not the only one who was silent. From the trees where they picked up Hugo back into town was two miles, and Blood and Linford's complaining at being forced to trot behind the wagon had lasted less than half a mile. As Billy towed them into the sheriff's office, the only sounds any of them made were gasps and coughs.

Billy's spirits were high. Blood would hang. With his own eyes, Billy had watched the man rob a train, murder four people, and attempt to murder more. There was no question in Billy's mind that Blood had also killed Cal Unger, but there was no proof.

As far as Lovett and the others were concerned, Billy knew Blood would never say anything to implicate them. Like Hugo said, Blood had no loyalty for anyone, but Billy knew the killer would never give the law the satisfaction.

So, it was unfortunate, but Lovett, McCutcheon, and Cooke would be convicted of nothing more than conspiracy to bribe public officials. It should be more, Billy knew, but he was glad for what he had.

Blood would die. That was the most important thing.

For the first time since seeing Frank's dead body, the slicing pain Billy experienced that day beside the tracks began to ease. That empty space began to fill. It wasn't gone. Billy doubted it would ever fill all the way, but it was better.

As they passed through the outer office, Billy grabbed the keys from the top of the sheriff's desk and led his three prisoners through the small room where Walter lay on the cot, sleeping.

"Right this way, gents," Billy said, and slammed each one into a cage. They collapsed onto their bunks, but none of them took their eyes from Billy.

Billy didn't mind their stares. Particularly Blood's. He took pleasure in them. It was the empty scrutiny of beaten men.

"Billy," Walt said as he came into the cell block, "you got 'em."

"I did," Billy said. "Hugo's outside. He's been wounded, and I'm going to take him to the doc's. You come along too. We'll have him look at your head."

"I'm all right," Walter said, but he was unconvincing. "I feel better now that I was able to sleep."

"Well, you don't look so good," Billy said. "The doctor should check you out."

Billy glanced at McCutcheon and Cooke. Like the others, these men stared at him, too. When he met their eyes, they diverted their gaze from Billy across the aisle to Lovett.

"Something interesting happened while you were gone, Billy," Walter said.

"What's that?"

"Shortly after you left, I was trying to sleep, but my head was hurting so bad I couldn't. Plus, I kept hearing these two whispering back and forth." He lifted his chin toward Cooke and McCutcheon.

"Whispering?"

"Right. This one—" He indicated McCutcheon. "—was saying maybe Henry Lovett had gone too far when he ordered Blood to kill Unger."

"What?" Billy asked.

McCutcheon came to his feet and so did Lovett. "That's a goddamned lie," McCutcheon shouted.

"That's right," Walter said, "McCutcheon was saying how Lovett ordered Blood to kill Unger and make it look like an accident. He told him to kill Bernard Simms and make it seem like just another murder during the train robbery." Walter stopped and rubbed his chin, searching his memory. "How was it he phrased it?" Walt had washed the blood from his head, but his wound was swollen and Billy could see the torn stitches.

211

"Just a second," Walter said. He left the cell block and stepped into the room containing the cot, table, and chair. When he returned, he was carrying a dozen sheets of writing paper. "Wait," said Walt, shuffling the papers, "let me find it. Here it is. McCutcheon was talking to Cooke, and he said, 'We both know, Fred, Henry went too far when he ordered Blood to kill everyone on the damned train. Maybe it would've looked suspicious just killing Simms and no one else, but there must've been another way.' "

Billy glanced at the papers in Walter's hand. They contained the same sorts of swirls and squiggles he'd first seen in Bernard Simms's notebook.

"My God," Billy said, taking the papers from him, "Walt, did you write Cooke and McCutcheon's conversation down in shorthand?"

Walter smiled. "Yes, I did. Oh, I might've missed the first couple of minutes or so, but I got the juicy parts."

Billy laughed. "By God, I'd say they're juicy—juicy enough to put Lovett on the gallows next to Blood." He turned to Lovett. "I swear, Mr. Lovett, when it comes to court reporters, you do have the worst kind of luck."

Hugo Dorling was still roaring drunk when Walt and Billy hoisted him out of the buckboard into the doctor's office. He sobered up fast, though, once the doc started working on his wounds. By the time the doctor was done, Hugo was as sober as a Sunday school teacher.

While the doctor worked on Walter in the next room, Billy sat beside Hugo's bed trying his best to roll the man a cigarette.

"Here, give me them makin's, for Chrissake. How can a fella be as old as you and not know how to roll a shuck?" Despite Hugo's groggy condition, he got the cigarette twisted up in no time. Billy, whose matches were in his saddlebag, dug one from the pocket of Hugo's jeans, which were draped across a chair in the corner. He struck the match on his gun butt as he came back across the room. Bending, he lit Hugo's cigarette.

Hugo sent a stream of smoke toward the ceiling and said, "So tell me about the events at the ranch house."

Billy provided a speedy version.

"You done good, son," Hugo said after Billy had told the story.

"I was ready to kill him, Hugo."

"I know you were. What's more, Zeke Blood knew it, too."

"And I would have done it gladly."

"Blood knew that as well. The way things was, you with your gun leveled, even as fast as he is, he had no chance of killin' you before you kilt him, unless he was able to spook you with his talk and cause you to slip up. When he saw you was not only ready to kill him, but you was eager to do it and would take pleasure in it to boot, he knew his chance of survival was slim."

Billy shook his head. "Take pleasure in it," he repeated. "I don't know, Hugo. I figure even in those dark places you mentioned, we should fight those feelings if we can."

Hugo seemed about to say something—explain a lifetime of choices, perhaps—but instead he stopped himself and only nodded. He dropped the stub of his smoke into the bed pan on the floor and settled back against his pillows.

"I'm convinced now that not killing Blood was a good thing," Billy added. "Maybe it balances out some of the bad that happened beside the tracks."

The two men sat awhile without speaking. Billy had nothing more to say.

After a bit, Hugo shut his eyes and pinched the bridge of his nose. "Damn, I don't know which is more powerful, Zeke Blood's Winchester or a fifth of Kentuck whiskey. It's a horrible thing to be both shot and hungover all at the same time."

Billy squeezed his old friend's arm, and pushed himself up from his chair. "You get some sleep, Hugo. In the morning, if the doc says it's okay, I'll get us seats on the afternoon train for Casper. I'll need to book three tickets and make horse-car arrangements for our mounts. Once we get you and Walter home, you boys can heal up proper." Billy turned for the door.

"Where you headed now?" Hugo asked.

"I thought I'd go over to Mrs. Jordan's Boarding House."

"Boardin' house? Kinda late, ain't it?" The thrifty Hugo wagged a finger. "Don't you let the widow charge you full price. The night's more than half over."

"Half over or not," Billy said, "a soft bed sounds fine. Mostly the reason I'm headed over there, though, is regarding the trip back to Casper."

"The trip? What about it?"

Billy opened the door to Hugo's room. As he stepped into the hallway, he looked back over his shoulder. "I need to speak to Jill Springer," he said with a smile. "I might have to buy one more ticket for the ride home tomorrow."

ABOUT THE AUTHOR

Robert McKee has had a number of jobs in his life, including four years in the military. He has also been employed as a radio announcer, disc jockey, copywriter, court reporter, and municipal court judge.

After school in Texas, Bob settled in Wyoming, where he lived for over thirty years. He and his wife Kathy now make their home along the Front Range in Colorado.

His short fiction has appeared in more than twenty commercial and literary publications around the country. He is also a recipient of the Wyoming Art Council's Literary Fellowship Award, as well as a three-time first-place winner of Wyoming Writers, Incorporated's adult fiction contest, and a two-time first-place winner of the National Writers Association's short fiction contest.

One of his stories was selected to appear in the prestigious annual publication Best American Mystery Stories, edited that year by Senior Editor Otto Penzler and Visiting Editor Michael Connelly.

When not at his computer writing, Bob can be found rummaging through antique stores in search of vintage fountain pens or roaming the back roads of Wyoming and Colorado with his wife.